"I Think You Should Marry Me."

He said it so calmly, so matter-of-factly, that the meaning of his words took several seconds to sink in. Then she was sure that she must have heard him wrong, or he was playing some cruel joke. That any second he was going to laugh and say, "Gotcha!"

"I know it's fast," he said instead. "I mean, we barely know each other. But for the baby's sake I really think it's the logical next move."

My God, he was *serious*. He wanted to marry her. How was that even possible when only a few days ago it supposedly hadn't been an option?

"But...you want to be prime minister."

"Yes, but that isn't what's best for the baby. I'm going to be a father. From now on, I have to put his or her best interests first."

Dear Reader,

Welcome to book eight of my ROYAL SEDUCTIONS series, the story of Princess Anne Charlotte Amalia Alexander and the heir to the political throne of Thomas Isle, Samuel Baldwin.

I can hardly believe that this is my last book in the ROYAL SEDUCTIONS series. <sniff> It seems as though only yesterday I introduced you to the royal families of Morgan and Thomas Isle. Since then we've been through a lot together. Marriages of convenience, illegitimate heirs and secret babies...just to name a few. And now an unexpected pregnancy has the royal family reeling.

There is a consensus on Thomas Isle that royalty and politics do not mix well. Leave it to Anne and Sam to put that theory to the test. And though you may think you know these two, what's going on in their heads, things are not always what they seem. There are family tragedies, boundaries pushed to the limit and mysteries solved. And this book ends with a *bang*...literally.

But I don't want to give away *too* much....

Until next time, all my best,

Michelle

MICHELLE CELMER

EXPECTANT PRINCESS, UNEXPECTED AFFAIR

Published by Silhouette Books
America's Publisher of Contemporary Romance

SILHOUETTE BOOKS
®

ISBN-13: 978-0-373-73045-2

PLEASE RECYCLE
THIS PRODUCT IS RECYCLABLE

Recycling programs
for this product may
not exist in your area.

EXPECTANT PRINCESS, UNEXPECTED AFFAIR

Books by Michelle Celmer

MICHELLE CELMER

Bestselling author Michelle Celmer lives in southeastern Michigan with her husband, their three children, two dogs and two cats. When she's not writing or busy being a mom, you can find her in the garden or curled up with a romance novel. And if you twist her arm really hard you can usually persuade her into a day of power shopping.

Michelle loves to hear from readers. Visit her Web site, www.michellecelmer.com, or write her at P.O. Box 300, Clawson, MI 48017.

To mothers and fathers, brothers and sisters, family and friends. Cherish your loved ones and keep them close. You never know what tomorrow will bring…

One

June

Though she had always considered her reserved nature one of her best qualities, there were times when Princess Anne Charlotte Amalia Alexander wished she could be more like her twin sister.

She sipped her champagne and watched from across the ballroom as Louisa approached one of the guests: a tall, dark and handsome gentleman who had been eyeing Louisa all evening. She smiled, said a few words, and he kissed her proffered hand.

It was so easy for her. Men were naturally drawn to her delicate beauty and enthralled by her childlike innocence.

But Anne? Men considered her cold and critical. It was no secret that people in society, men in particular, often referred to her as *The Shrew*. Usually she didn't let that bother her. She liked to believe that they felt threatened by her strength and independence. However, that was little consolation on a night like this one. Everyone around her was dancing and drinking and socializing, while she stood by herself, alone in her principles. But with her father's failing health, was it so hard to fathom that she just didn't *feel* like celebrating?

A waiter carrying a tray of champagne passed by and she snagged a fresh glass. Her fourth for that night, which was precisely three more than she normally drank.

Her father, the king of Thomas Isle, who should at least be able to attend the charity event they were holding in his honor, was too weakened by heart disease to even make an appearance. Her mother refused to leave his side. It was up to Anne, Louisa and their brothers, Chris and Aaron, to act as hosts in the king's absence.

Getting hammered probably wasn't in her or the rest of the family's best interest. But didn't Anne always do as she was told? Wasn't she always the rational, responsible twin?

Well, almost always.

She knocked back the champagne in two swallows, deposited her empty glass on another passing tray and grabbed a fresh one. She would drink this one slower, she promised herself, but already she could feel the alcohol warming her belly and she began to get a soft, fuzzy feeling in her head. It was…nice.

She downed glass number five in one long swallow.

"You're looking lovely, Your Highness," someone said from behind her.

She turned to the voice, surprised to find Samuel Baldwin, son of the prime minister of Thomas Isle, greeting her. Sam was the sort of man a women looked at and instantly went weak in the knees. At thirty he was more cute than handsome—at least she thought so—with naturally curly, dark blond hair that never seemed to behave and deep dimples in both cheeks when he smiled. He was several inches taller than her own five foot eight, with a lean, muscular build. She had spoken to him a time or two, but nothing more than a casual hello. The gossip mill pegged him as one of the island's most eligible bachelors, and he had been groomed since birth to take over his father's position.

He bowed in greeting, and as he did, a lock of that unruly hair fell across his forehead. Anne resisted the urge to reach up and brush it back, but couldn't help wondering what it would feel like to run her fingers through it.

She would normally greet him with cool indifference, but the alcohol was doing funny things to her head because she could feel herself smiling. "How nice to see you again, Mr. Baldwin."

"Please," he said, "call me Sam."

Out of the corner of her eye Anne saw Louisa on the dance floor, her mystery man holding her scandalously close, gazing into her eyes. A pang of jealousy soured Anne's stomach. She wanted a man to hold her close and look at her as though she were the only one in the room, as if he couldn't wait to get her alone so he could ravage her. Just this once she wanted to feel…wanted. Was that really too much to ask for?

She finished her champagne in one gulp and asked, "Would you care to dance, Sam?"

She wasn't sure if his look of surprise was due to her barbaric behavior, or the actual invitation. For a dreadfully long and horrifying instant, she thought he might turn her down. Wouldn't that be ironic considering all the dance invitations she had declined over the years? So many, in fact, that men had stopped asking altogether.

Then a grin curled his mouth, his dimples a prominent dent in each cheek, and he said, "I would be honored, Your Highness."

He offered his arm and she slipped hers through it. Then he led her out onto the crowded dance floor. It had been so long since she'd danced that when he took her in his arms and began to waltz, what used to be second nature suddenly felt clumsy and awkward. Or maybe that was the champagne making her knees soft…or the spicy scent of his aftershave making her light-headed. He smelled so delicious, she wanted to bury her face in the crook of his neck and breathe him in. She tried to recall the last time she'd been this close to a man she found so sexually appealing.

Maybe a little *too* long.

"Black suits you," Sam said, and it took her several seconds to realize he was talking about her gown, a floor-length, sequined number she had purchased off the rack in Paris. She didn't know if the color suited her so much as it had suited her mood when she'd picked it out. Now she wished she had worn something brighter and more cheerful. Like Louisa in her trademark pink, who, come to think of it, looked a bit like the Good Witch of the North. Which Anne supposed would make her the Wicked Witch of the West.

"Yes," she told Sam. "All that's missing is the pointy black hat."

It was the sort of remark that might put a man off. Instead Sam laughed. A deep, throaty laugh that seemed to vibrate through her, causing delicious friction that warmed her insides. "Actually, I was thinking that it brings out your milky complexion."

"Oh, well, thank you."

A slow song began, and Anne couldn't help noticing how Louisa's mystery man drew her in even closer. A little *too* close.

"Do you know that man dancing with my sister?" she asked Sam, gesturing with her chin.

"Garrett Sutherland. He's the richest landowner on the island. I'm surprised you don't know him."

The name was definitely familiar. "I know *of* him. I've heard my brothers mention him."

"It looks as though he and your sister are quite… friendly."

"I noticed that, too."

He watched Anne watching her sister. "You look out for her?"

She nodded and looked up at him. "Someone has to. She can be very naive, and far too trusting."

He grinned, his dimples so adorable she wanted to rise up and press a kiss to each one. "Then who looks after you?"

"No one needs to. I'm entirely capable of looking out for myself."

He tightened the arm around her back, tucking her

closer to his chest, and his smile went from teasing to sizzling. "Are you sure about that, Highness?"

Was he *flirting* with her? Men never teased and flirted with her. Not unless they wanted their head handed back to them on a platter. Samuel Baldwin was a brave man. And she realized, she *liked* it. She liked the weight of his hand on her back and the way it felt when her breasts skimmed the wall of his chest. She'd never been what anyone could call a sexual woman—not that she didn't enjoy a quick, meaningless roll in the hay now and then—but being close to Sam awakened feelings in her she never knew were there. Or was it more the champagne than the man?

No. No amount of alcohol had ever given her this warm, shivery, feverish ache. This primitive longing to be taken and…possessed. To rip Sam's clothes off and put her hands all over him. She wondered what he would do if she wrapped her arms around his neck, tugged his head down and kissed him. His lips looked so soft and sensual and she was dying to know what they would feel like, how they would taste.

She wished she possessed the courage to do it, right here, right now, in front of all these people. She wished she could be more like Louisa, who was now walking arm in arm with her dance partner, out the doors and onto the patio, seemingly oblivious to the hundred or so pairs of eyes following their every move.

Maybe it was about time Louisa learned to fend for herself. For tonight at least. From this moment forward, she was on her own.

Anne turned her attention to Sam and smiled. "I'm

so pleased you could attend our benefit. Are you having a good time?"

"I am. I was sorry to hear that the king wasn't well enough to attend."

"He has to have a procedure done and adjustments made to his heart pump so he must stay in tip-top shape. Being in a large crowd could expose him to infection. His system is very vulnerable."

Her siblings all seemed to think he was going to be fine, and the heart pump he had been attached to for the past nine months was going to give his damaged heart the time it needed to heal, but Anne had a bad feeling it was a waste of time. Lately he'd begun to look so pale and he had so little energy. She worried that he was losing his will to live.

Though the rest of the family was hopeful, deep down Anne knew he was going to die and her instincts were telling her that it would be soon.

A sudden feeling of intense grief welled up inside her, and hard as she tried to push it back down, tears sprang to the corners of her eyes and a sob began to build in her throat. She never got upset, at least not when other people were around to see it, but the champagne must have compromised her emotions because she was on the verge of a meltdown and she couldn't do a single thing to stop it.

Not here, she begged. *Please not in front of all these people.*

"Anne, are you okay?" Sam was gazing down at her, his eyes so full of concern and compassion, it was almost too much.

She bit down hard on her lip and shook her head, and he seemed to know exactly what to do.

He swiftly whisked her off the dance floor, while she struggled to maintain her composure. "Where to?" he whispered, as they exited the ballroom, into a foyer full of people socializing and sipping drinks. She needed to be somewhere private, where no one would see the inevitable breakdown. A place where, when she finally pulled herself together, she could fix her makeup and return to the party as though nothing were out of the ordinary.

"My room," she managed.

"Upstairs?" he asked, and she nodded. She was biting her lip so hard now she tasted blood.

The staircase was roped off and two security officers stood guard, but as they approached one unhooked the rope to let them pass.

"Her Highness was kind enough to offer me a tour of the castle," Sam told them, which really wasn't necessary. Then she realized he'd said it not for the guards' sake, but for the guests who were watching them. She would have to remember to thank him. But the fact that he cared about her reputation, that he would be so kind as to help her avoid embarrassment, brought the tears even closer to the surface. They were halfway up to the second floor when her eyes started to leak rivers of warm tears down her cheeks, and when they reached her door and he ushered her inside, the floodgates burst.

She thought for sure he would leave her alone, but after she heard the door close Sam's arms went around her, pulling her tight against him. The idea that he cared enough to stay, when normally she felt so isolated in her grief, made her cry even harder.

Anne clung to him, sobbing her heart out against his chest, both mortified and desperately grateful that he was there.

"Let it out, Annie," he whispered, rubbing her back and stroking her hair. No one but Louisa had called her Annie, and it made her feel close to him somehow, which made no sense because she barely knew him. Still it felt as if they had shared something special. Something intimate.

As spontaneous and intense as the emotional outburst had been, it was surprisingly short-lived. As the sobs subsided, Sam handed her his handkerchief and she dabbed her eyes.

"She cries," he said, sounding amazed.

"Please don't tell anyone," she whispered against his jacket.

"They wouldn't believe me if I did."

Of course they wouldn't. She was the ice princess, *The Shrew*. She didn't have feelings. But the truth was she felt just as deeply as anyone else, she was just damned good at hiding it. But she didn't want to be the ice princess anymore. At least, not tonight. Tonight she wanted someone to know the woman underneath.

Sam cradled her face in his palms and gently tipped it up to his, wiping the last of her tears away with his thumbs. She gazed up into eyes as clear blue as the ocean, and she could swear she felt something shift deep inside her.

She wasn't sure if he made the first move, or she did, or they met halfway, but suddenly their lips were locked, and in that instant she had never wanted a man more than she wanted him.

Any man who accused Princess Anne of being cold and unfeeling had obviously never kissed her. She tasted sweet and salty, like champagne and tears, and she put her heart and soul, her entire being into it.

Though Sam wasn't quite sure who kissed whom first, he had the feeling he might have just unleashed some sort of wild animal. She clawed at his clothes, yanking his jacket off his shoulders and down his arms, tugging his bow tie loose. She fumbled with his belt, unfastened his pants, and before he could manage to catch his breath, slid her hand inside his boxers and wrapped it around him. Sam cursed under his breath, a word that under normal circumstances he would never dare utter in the presence of royalty, but he was having one hell of a tough time reconciling the princess he knew with the wild woman who was now walking backward toward her bed, unzipping her dress and letting it fall to the floor. She plucked a jewel-encrusted comb from her hair and he watched as it spilled down over her shoulders like black silk. She grinned wickedly, tempting him with eyes the color of the sky just before a storm—smoky gray and turbulent.

Though under normal circumstances he would find it juvenile and downright rude, when his mates dared Sam to ask Princess Anne, *The Shrew,* to dance, he'd had just enough champagne to take the bait. But never in a million years did he expect her to ask him first. Nor did he expect to find himself in her bedroom, Anne undressed to her black lace strapless bra and matching panties. And as she draped her long, lithe body across the mattress, summoning him closer with a crooked finger and a seductive smile, he guessed it wouldn't be long before she wore nothing at all.

"Take your clothes off," she demanded as she reached around behind her to unhook her bra. Her breasts were small and firm and he could hardly wait to get his hands on them, to taste them. He ripped his shirt off, losing a button or two in his haste, then stepped out of his pants, grabbing his wallet for later. That was when he realized the mistake he'd made and cursed again.

"What's wrong?" Anne asked.

"I don't have a condom."

"You don't?" she said, looking crestfallen.

He shook his head. It wasn't as if he came to these events expecting to shag, and even if he had, he would have anticipated taking the woman in question home, where he kept an entire box in his bedside table drawer.

"I've got it covered," Anne told him.

"You have a condom?"

"No, but I have it covered."

In other words, she was on birth control, but that wouldn't protect either of them from disease. But he knew he was clean, and it was a safe bet to assume she was, too. So why not? Besides, Anne was wearing a look that said she wouldn't be taking no for an answer.

He dropped the rest of his clothes in a pile and joined her. As she dragged him down onto the bed, ravaging his mouth with a deep, desperate kiss, rolling him onto his back and straddling him, he had the feeling this was a night he wouldn't soon forget.

They had barely gotten started and it was already the best sex he'd ever had.

Two

September

I've got it covered, Anne thought wryly as she dragged herself up from the bathroom floor, still weak and shaky, and propped herself against the vanity over the sink. What the bloody hell had she been thinking when she told Sam that? Had she not bothered to even consider the consequences? The repercussions of her actions?

Well, she was considering them now. And she had no one to blame but herself.

She rinsed her mouth and splashed cold water on her face and the wave of nausea began to pass. The family physician, whom she had sworn to total secrecy, had assured her that she'd feel better in her second trimester. But here she was in her fifteenth week, three weeks past that magical date, and she still felt like the walking dead.

But it was worth it, she thought, as she laid a hand over the tiny bump that had begun to form just below her navel.

It was hard to believe that at first, when she learned she was pregnant, she wasn't even sure that she wanted to keep it. Her initial plan had been to take an extended vacation somewhere remote and warm, live in exile until it was born, and then give it up for adoption. Then Chris's wife, Melissa, had given birth to their triplets and Anne cradled her tiny niece and nephews in her arms for the first time. Despite never having given much thought to having children—it had always seemed so far off in the future—in that instant she knew she wanted her baby. She wanted someone to love her unconditionally. Someone to depend on her.

She was going to have this baby and she was going to raise it herself. With support from her family, of course. Which she was sure she would get just as soon as she told them. So far only her twin sister, Louisa, knew. As for Sam, he obviously wanted nothing to do with her.

Their night together had been like a fantasy come to life. She'd heard her sister talk for years about destiny and finding one true love. And in fact, Louisa's dreams had come true at the ball—she was now married to her mystery man, Garrett Sutherland. But until Sam kissed Anne, until he made love to her so passionately, until, exhausted, they fell asleep in each other's arms, Anne hadn't truly believed in love. But now that she did, it would seem that Sam didn't share her feelings.

She had been sure that it had been as special for him as it had been for her, that they had connected on some deeply visceral level. Even when she had woken up alone and realized that at some time in the night he had slipped away without saying goodbye, she wouldn't let her hopes be dashed. She kept waiting to hear from him. For weeks she stayed close to the phone, willing it to ring, hoping to answer and hear his voice. But the call never came.

She shouldn't have been surprised, really. Sam was a politician, and everyone knew that politics and royalty did not mix well. Not if Sam wanted to be prime minister someday, and that was what she'd heard. By law, no member of the royal family was permitted to hold a position in government. Could she honestly blame him for choosing a career he had spent his entire life preparing for over her? That was why she had made the decision not to tell him about the baby. It was a complication that neither of them needed. And one she was quite sure he didn't want despite the scandal it would cause for her.

She could see the headlines now. *Princess Anne Pregnant with Secret Love Child.*

No matter how liberal the world had become in such matters, she was royalty and held to a higher standard. The stigma would follow her and, even worse, her child, for the rest of their lives. But at this point, she saw no other options.

Feeling half-human again, she decided she should get back to the dining room and try to choke down a few bites of dinner. Geoffrey, their butler, had just begun to serve the first course when her stomach lurched and she'd had to excuse herself and dash to the loo.

She gave one last furtive look in the mirror and decided that short of a total makeover, this was as good as it was going to get. She opened the door and almost collided with her brother Chris, who was leaning against the wall just outside.

Bloody hell.

His grim expression said that he had heard her retching, and he wanted to know what would cause her to be so ill.

"Let's have a talk," he said, jerking his head toward the study across the hall.

"But, supper…" she started to say, and he gave her that *look*.

"*Now,* Anne."

Since arguing would be a waste of time, she followed him. With their father in poor health, Chris was acting king, and technically the head of the family. She was duty-bound to follow his lead. And didn't she always do as she was told? Wouldn't everyone be surprised when they learned of her predicament.

She could lie and tell him that she had a flu bug, or a mild case of food poisoning, but at the rate her tummy was swelling, it wouldn't be long before it was impossible to hide anyway. But she wasn't sure if she was ready for the truth to come out just yet.

Or maybe he already knew. Had Louisa blabbed? Anne would kill her if that was the case.

Anne stepped into the study, and, shy of her mother, father and the triplets, the entire family was there!

Aaron and his wife, Liv, a botanical geneticist, sat on the couch looking worried. Louisa and her new husband, Garrett, stood across the room by the window. Louisa wore a pained expression and Garrett looked as though he wanted to be anywhere but there. Melissa, Chris's wife, stood just inside the door, looking anxious. Not five minutes ago they had all been in the dinning room eating supper.

Her first instinct was to turn and walk right back out, but Chris had already followed her in and shut the door.

What a nightmare.

"I don't suppose I have to tell you why I asked you here," he said.

Ordered was more like it. Now she was sorry she'd agreed.

"We're very concerned," Melissa said, walking over to stand beside Chris. "You haven't been yourself lately, Anne. For the last couple of months you've been pale and listless. Not to mention all the times you've dashed off to the loo."

So they didn't know. Louisa had kept her secret.

"It's obvious something is wrong," Aaron said. He normally wasn't one to butt into other people's business, so she knew he must have been genuinely concerned. Maybe waiting so long to tell everyone had been an error in judgment. She didn't honestly think that anyone really noticed the changes in her or for that matter cared about them.

"If you're ill—" Melissa began.

"I'm not ill," Anne assured her.

"An eating disorder is a disease," Chris said.

Anne turned to him, amused because Louisa had suspected the same thing at first. "Chris, if I were bulimic, I would be dashing off to the loo after supper, not before."

He didn't look as though he believed her. "I know something is wrong."

"It all depends on how you look at it, I guess."

"Look at what?" Melissa asked.

Just tell them, dummy. "I'm pregnant."

All through the room jaws dropped. Except Louisa's, of course.

"If this is some kind of joke, I'm not amused," Chris said.

"It's no joke."

"Of course!" Melissa said, as though the lightbulb had just flashed on. "I should have realized. I just never thought..."

"I would be careless enough to go out and get myself in trouble?" Anne asked.

"I...I wasn't even aware that you were seeing anyone," Aaron said.

"I'm not. It was a one-time encounter."

"Maybe this is a silly question," Chris said. "But are you sure? Have you taken a test? Seen the family physician?"

She lifted the hem of the cardigan she'd been wearing to hide the evidence and smoothed her dress down over her bump. "What do you think?"

Had his eyes not been fastened in they might have fallen out of his head. "Good God, how far along are you?"

"Fifteen weeks."

"You're *four* months pregnant and you never thought to mention it?"

"I planned to announce it when the time was right."

"When? After your water broke?" he snapped, and Melissa put a hand on his arm to calm him.

"There's no need to get snippy," Anne said.

Ironic coming from her, his look said, the princess of snip. Well, maybe she didn't want to be that way any longer. Maybe she was tired of always being on the defensive.

"This isn't like you, Anne," Chris said.

"It's not as if I went out and got knocked up on purpose, you know." Although he was right. She had been uncharacteristically irresponsible.

I've got it covered. Brilliant.

"This is going to be a nightmare when it hits the press," Melissa said. Being an illegitimate princess herself, she would certainly know. Until recently she'd lived in the U.S., unaware that she was heir to the throne of Morgan Isle.

"And what about the Gingerbread Man?" Louisa asked, speaking up for the first time. "I'm sure he'll use the opportunity to try to scare us."

The self-proclaimed Gingerbread Man was the extremely disturbed man who had been harassing the royal family for more than a year. He began by hacking their computer system and sending Anne and her siblings twisted and grisly versions of fairy tales, then he breached security on the palace grounds to leave an ominous note. Not long after, posing as housekeeping staff, he'd made it as far as the royal family's private waiting room at the hospital. Hours after he was gone, security found the chilling calling card he'd left behind. An envelope full of photographs of Anne and her siblings that the Gingerbread Man had taken in various places so they would know that he was there, watching.

He would sometimes be silent for months, yet every time they thought they had heard the last of him, he would reappear out of the blue. He sent a basket of rotten fruit for Christmas and an e-mail congratulating Chris and Melissa about the triplets before her pregnancy had even been formally announced.

His most recent stunt had been breaking into the florist the night before Aaron and Liv's wedding in March and spraying the flowers with something that had caused them to wilt just in time for the ceremony.

Anne was sure he would pull something when he learned of her pregnancy, but she refused to let him get to her. She wouldn't give him the satisfaction. "I don't care what the Gingerbread Man does," she said, lifting her chin in defiance. "Personally, I'm all for drawing him out into the open so he makes a mistake and gets caught."

"Which we have agreed not to do," Chris said sternly.

Aaron asked the next obvious question. "What about the father of the baby? Is he taking responsibility?"

"Like I said, it was a one-night thing."

Chris frowned. "He didn't offer to marry you?"

This was where it was going to get tricky. "No. Besides, he's not a royal."

"I don't give a damn who he is. He needs to take responsibility for his actions."

"Liv and Garrett aren't royals. And I'm only half-royal," Melissa added.

"It doesn't matter. He's out of the picture," Anne insisted.

"And that was his choice?" Aaron asked.

Anne bit her lip.

"Anne?" Chris asked, and when she remained silent he cursed under his breath. "He doesn't know, does he?"

"Trust me when I say, he's better off."

Melissa made a clucking noise, as though she were thoroughly disappointed in Anne.

"That is not your decision to make," Chris said. "I don't care who he is, he has a right to know he's going to have a child. To keep it from him is unconscionable."

She knew deep down that he was right. But she was feeling hurt and bitter and stubborn. If Sam didn't want her, why should he be allowed access to their child?

"Sam may be a politician, but he's a good man," Chris said.

Once again, mouths fell open in surprise, including her own. She hadn't told anyone the father's identity. Not even Louisa. "How did you—"

"Simple math. You don't honestly think Melissa and I could go through months of infertility treatments and a high-risk pregnancy without learning a thing or two about getting pregnant? Conception would have had to have occurred around the time of the charity ball. And do you really think that Sam's sneaking out in the middle of the night would go unnoticed?"

No, of course not. They were under a ridiculously tight lockdown these days. "You never said anything."

"What was I supposed to say? You're a grown woman. As long as you're discreet, who you sleep with is your business." He put both hands on her shoulders. "But now, you need to call him and set up a meeting."

"Why, so you can have a *talk* with him?"

"No. So *you* can. Because it's not only unfair to Sam, it's unfair to that baby you're carrying. He or she deserves the chance to know their father. If that's what Sam wants."

"He's right," Louisa said. "Put yourself in Sam's place."

"You should definitely tell him the truth," Aaron said.

She fiddled with the hem of her sweater, unable to meet Chris's eyes, knowing he was right. If not for Sam, then for the baby's sake. "I'm not sure what to say to him."

"Well," Melissa said. "I often find it's best to start with the truth."

Sam had just ended a call with the Secretary of State of DFID, or what the Brits called the Department for International Development, when his secretary, Grace, rang him.

"You have a visitor, sir."

A visitor? He didn't recall any appointments on the calendar for this afternoon. This was typically his time for any calls that needed to be made. Had Grace scheduled another appointment she'd forgotten to mention? Or maybe she had entered information incorrectly into the computer again.

He was sure at one time she had been an asset to his father's office, but now she was at least ten years past mandatory retirement.

"Do they have an appointment?" he asked her.

"No, sir, but—"

"Then I don't have time. I'll be happy to see them after they schedule an appointment." He hung up, wishing he could gently persuade his father to let her go, or at the very least assign her to someone else. But she had been with the office since the elder Baldwin was a young politician just starting out and he was as fiercely loyal to her as she was to him. Sam may have suspected some sort of indiscretion had it not been for the fact that she was fifteen years his father's senior, and they were both very happily married to other people.

There was a knock at his office door and Sam groaned inwardly, gathering every bit of his patience. Did Grace not understand the meaning of the word *no?* "What is it?" he snapped, probably a bit more harshly than she deserved.

The door opened, but it wasn't Grace standing there. It was Anne. *Princess* Anne, he reminded himself. Spending one night in her bed did not give him the privilege of dispensing with formalities.

"Your Highness," he said, rising from his chair and bowing properly, even though he couldn't help picturing her naked and poised atop him, her breasts firm and high, her face a mask of pleasure as she rode him until they were both blind with ecstasy. To say they'd slept together, that they'd had sex, was like calling the ocean a puddle. They had transcended every preconceived notion he'd ever had about being with a woman. It was a damned shame that they had no future.

He must have picked up the phone a dozen times to call her in the weeks following their night together, but before he could dial he'd been faced with a grim reality. No matter how he felt about her, how deeply they had connected, if he wanted to be prime minister, he simply could not have her.

He had accepted a long time ago that getting where he wanted would involve sacrifice. Yet never had it hit home so thoroughly as it did now.

"Is this a bad time?" she asked.

"No, of course not. Come in, please."

She stepped into his office and shut the door behind her. Though she was, on most occasions, coolly composed, today she seemed edgy and nervous, her eyes flitting randomly about his office. Looking everywhere, he noticed, but at him.

"I'm sorry to just barge in on you this way. But I was afraid that if I called you might refuse to see me."

"You're welcome anytime, Your Highness." He came around his desk and gestured to the settee and chair in the sitting area. "Please, have a seat. Can I get you a drink?"

"No, thank you. I'm fine." She sat primly on the edge of the settee, clutching her purse in her lap, and he took a seat in the chair. She looked thinner than when he'd last seen her, and her milky complexion had taken on a gray cast. Was she ill?

"Maybe just a glass of water?" he asked.

She shook her head, her lips folded firmly together, and he watched as her face went from gray to green before his eyes. Then her eyes went wide, and she asked in a panicked voice, "The loo?"

He pointed across the room. "Just through that—"

She was up off the settee, one hand clamped over her

mouth, dashing for the door before he could even finish his sentence. It might have been comedic had he not been so alarmed. He followed her and stood outside the door, cringing when he heard the sounds of her being ill. There was obviously something terribly wrong with her. But why come to him? They barely knew one another. On a personal level at any rate.

He heard a flush, then the sound of water running.

"Should I call someone for you?" he asked, then the door opened and Anne emerged looking pale and shaky.

"No, I'm fine. Just dreadfully embarrassed. I should have known better than to eat before I came here."

"Why don't you sit down." He reached out to help her but she waved him away.

"I can do it." She crossed the room on wobbly legs and re-staked her seat on the settee. Sam sat in the chair.

"Forgive me for being blunt, Your Highness, but are you ill?"

"Sam, we've been about as intimate as two people can be, so please call me Anne. And no, I'm not ill. Not in the way you might think."

"In what way, then?"

She took a deep breath and blew it out. "I'm pregnant."

"Pregnant?" he repeated, and she nodded. Well, he hadn't seen that coming. He'd barely been able to look at another woman without seeing Anne's face, but it would seem she'd had no trouble moving on. And what reason had he given her not to? Maybe that night hadn't been as fantastic for her as it was for him. It would explain why she had made no attempt to contact him afterward.

But if she was happy, he would be happy for her. "I hadn't heard. Congratulations."

She looked at him funny, then said, "I'm four months."

Four months? He counted back and realized that their night together had been almost exactly—

Sam's gut tightened.

"Yes, it's yours," she said.

He *really* hadn't seen *that* coming. "You're sure?"

She nodded. "There hasn't been anyone else. Not after, and not a long time before."

"I thought you said you had it covered."

"I guess nothing is one hundred percent guaranteed."

Apparently not.

"If you require a DNA test—"

"No," he said. "I trust your word." What reason did she have to lie?

They were going to have a baby. He and the princess. He was going to be a *father*.

He had always planned to have a family someday, but not until he was a bit more established in his career. And not until he met the right woman.

"You're probably wondering why I waited so long to tell you," she said.

Among other things. "Why did you?"

"I just…I didn't want to burden you with this. I didn't want you to feel…obligated. Which I realize now was totally unfair of me. And I apologize. I just want you to know that I don't expect anything from you. I'm fully prepared to raise this baby on my own. Whether or not you want to be a part of its life is your choice entirely."

What kind of man did she take him to be? "Let's get one thing perfectly clear," he told her. "This is my *child,* and I'm going to be a part of it's life."

"Of course," she said softly. "I wasn't sure. Some men—"

"I am *not* some men," he told her firmly. "I hope that won't be a problem for you or your family."

She shook her head. "No, of course not. I think it's wonderful. A child should have both its parents."

He leaned back in the chair, shaking his head. "I'm... *wow.* This is quite a surprise."

"I can relate, believe me. This was not the way I imagined starting a family."

"I suppose some sort of announcement will have to be made." He could just imagine what his friends would say. For weeks after the ball they had tried to bully him into explaining his and the princess's sudden absence from the party, but he'd refused to say a word. Now everyone would know. Not that he was embarrassed or ashamed of what he'd done. "You know that the press will be brutal."

"I know. When they learn you're the father and that we're not...together, they won't leave us alone."

If that was some sort of hint as to the future direction of their relationship, he hated to disappoint her, but he was not about to give up everything he had worked so hard for, his lifelong dream, for a one-night stand.

He cared for Anne, lusted after her even, but a marriage was absolutely out of the question.

Three

"The press will just have to get used to the idea of us being friends," Sam told her.

"I hope we can be, for the baby's sake."

"And your family? How do they feel about this?"

"So far only my siblings know. They were surprised, but very supportive. My father's health is particularly fragile right now, so we've decided to wait to tell him and my mother. I have to admit that *you're* taking this much better than I expected. I thought you would be angry."

"It was an accident. What right would I have to be angry? You didn't force me."

"Didn't I?"

He wouldn't deny that she had started it, and she had been quite…*aggressive*. But he had been a willing participant. "Anne, we share equal responsibility."

"Not all men would feel that way."

"Yes, well, I'm not all men."

There was a short period of awkward silence, so he asked, "Everything is okay? With the pregnancy, I mean. You and the baby are healthy?"

"Oh yes," she said, instinctively touching a hand to her belly. "Everything's fine. I'm right on schedule."

"Do you know the sex of the baby?"

"Not for another month, at my next ultrasound." She paused, then said, "You could go, too. If you'd like."

"I would. Are you showing yet?"

"I have a little bump. Want to see?" She surprised him by lifting up the hem of her top and showing him her bare tummy. But why would she be shy when he had seen a lot more than just her stomach?

Her tummy had indeed swelled and was quite prominent considering how thin she was. He wasn't sure what possessed him, but he asked, "Can I touch it?"

"Of course," she said, gesturing him over.

He moved to the settee beside her and she took his hand, laying it on her belly. She was warm and soft there, and the familiar scent of her skin seemed to eat up all of the breathable air. His hand was so large that his fingers spanned the top of her bump all the way down to the top edge of her panties.

Maybe this wasn't such a good idea. Knowing they couldn't be together didn't make him want her any less. And knowing that it was his baby growing inside her gave him an almost irrational desire to protect her, to claim her as his own.

And hadn't he felt the same way the night they had made love?

"Have you felt it move?"

"Flutters mostly. No actual kicks yet. But press right here," she said, pushing his fingers more firmly against her belly, until he hit something firm and unyielding. She looked up at him and smiled, her mouth inches from his own. "You feel it?"

Did he ever, and it took all of his restraint not to lean in and capture her lips. He breathed in the scent of her hair, her skin, longing to taste her again, to...*take* her. But a sexual relationship at this stage, with her all hormones and emotions, could spell disaster.

She seemed to sense what he was thinking, because color suddenly flooded her cheeks and he could see the flutter of her pulse at the base of her neck. Without realizing it, he had started to lean in, and her chin had begun to lift, like the pull of a magnet drawing them together. But thank goodness he came to his senses at the last second and turned away. He pulled his hand from her belly and rose to his feet. His heart was hammering and she'd gone from looking pale and shaky to flushed and feverish.

"This is not a good idea," he said.

"You're right," she agreed, nodding vigorously. "I wasn't thinking."

"It would be in our best interest to keep this relationship platonic. Otherwise things could get confusing."

"Very confusing."

"Which could be a challenge," he admitted. Total honesty at this point only seemed fair, as she had been forthcoming with him. "It's obvious that I'm quite attracted to you."

"There does seem to be some sort of…connection."

That was putting it mildly. It was taking every bit of restraint he could gather to stop himself from taking her, right there in his office. Pregnant or not, he wanted to strip her naked and ravish her, drive into her until she screamed with release. The way she had that night in her bedroom. He'd never been with a woman so responsive to his touch, so easy to please. He couldn't help wondering if her pregnancy had changed that. He'd often heard that it made women even more receptive to physical stimulation. And maybe it was true, because he could clearly see the firm peaks of her nipples through her clothes. Her breasts looked larger than they had been before, too. Rounder and fuller. What would she do if he took one in his mouth…?

He swallowed hard and looked away, turning toward his desk, so she might not notice how aroused he was becoming. "You mentioned an ultrasound. Do you know the time and date, so I can mark it on my calendar?"

She rattled off the information and he slid into his chair behind the safety of his desk and made himself a note.

"Maybe we could have dinner this Friday," she said, then added quickly, "A platonic dinner, of course. So we can discuss how we plan to handle things. Like the press and custody."

That would give him three days to think this through and process it all. He always preferred to have a solid and well-considered plan of action before he entered into negotiations of any kind.

However, he wasn't sure he was ready to be thrown

in the mix with her family just yet. Not that he didn't feel as though he could hold his own. He just felt these matters were private, between himself and Anne, and in no way concerned her family.

"How about we eat at my place," he said. "Seven o'clock?"

"If you don't mind your residence being swarmed with security. We're still on high alert."

He frowned. "Is the royal family still being harassed?"

"Unfortunately, yes."

All he knew of the situation was what he'd read in the papers. "So it's serious," he said.

"More than anyone realizes, I'm afraid. There have been threats of violence against the family. I should probably warn you that once we're linked together, you could become a target, as well."

He shrugged. "I'm not worried. As far as the baby goes, I'm assuming that until you've told your father, there will be no announcement to the press."

"Of course not."

"I do intend to tell my family, but they can be trusted to keep it quiet."

"Of course you should tell them. Do you think they'll be upset?"

Her look of vulnerability surprised him. He didn't think she was afraid of anything. Or cared what anyone thought of her. But hadn't he learned that night at the ball that she wasn't nearly as tough as she liked people to believe? "I think they'll be surprised, but happy," he told her.

He just hoped it was true.

* * *

Sam stopped in to see his parents that evening to break the news. When he arrived they had just finished supper and were relaxing out on the veranda with snifters of brandy, watching the sun set. Despite his father's career in politics, and his mother's touring as an operatic vocalist, they always made time for each other. After forty years they were still happily married and going strong.

That was the sort of marriage Sam had always imagined for himself. He had just never met a woman he could see himself spending the rest of his life with. Until Anne, he admitted grudgingly. How ironic that when he finally found her, he couldn't have her.

He wasn't quite sure how they would react to learning that they would be grandparents to the next prince or princess of Thomas Isle, but under the circumstances, they took it pretty well. Probably in part because they had been vying for grandchildren for some time and Sam's older brother, Adam, had yet to deliver.

"I'm sure I'm going to sound old-fashioned," his mother said, "but ideally we would like to see you married."

"Mother—"

"However," she continued. "We understand that you need to do what you feel is right."

"If I married Anne, I would be considered a royal and I would never be prime minister. That isn't a sacrifice I'm willing to make." Of course, with that in mind, he shouldn't have slept with her in the first place, should he? He suspected that was what his mother was thinking.

"You would be giving your child a name," his father pointed out.

"I don't need to be married to do that. He had my name the moment he was conceived."

"He?" his mother asked, brows raised.

"Or she."

"Will you find out?"

"I'd like to. And I think Anne would, too. She has an ultrasound in four weeks."

"Maybe I could invite her for tea," she suggested, and at Sam's wary look added, "I should be allowed to get to know the mother of my future grandchild."

She was right. And he was sure Anne would be happy to oblige her. Didn't pregnant women love to talk about their condition with other women? Especially the grandparents? "I'll mention it to her."

"You know that this is going to be complicated," his father said. "They think differently than we do."

"They?"

"Royals."

"Not so different as you might expect," Sam said. "Not Anne, anyway. She's actually quite down-to-earth."

"I've only spoken briefly with the princess," his mother said. "But she seemed lovely."

There was a "however" hanging there, and Sam knew exactly what she was thinking. What they were *both* thinking. He couldn't deny he'd thought the same thing before his night with Anne. "I know you've probably heard things about her. Unfavorable things. But she isn't at all what you would expect. She's intelligent and engaging." And fantastic in bed...

"It sounds as if you're quite taken with her," his mother not-so-subtly hinted.

He was. Probably too much for his own good. He just hoped that once Anne began to look more pregnant, and especially after the baby was born, it would be easier for him to see her only as the mother of his child and not a sexual being.

"I have every hope that Anne and I can be good friends, for the child's sake, but that is as far as it will ever go."

He knew they were disappointed. This wasn't the sort of scenario his parents had envisioned for him, and honestly neither had he. He had assumed that it would have been like it had been for them. He would meet a woman and they would date for a reasonable period of time, then marry and have a family. Sam would eventually become prime minister, and his wife would have a rewarding and lucrative career that still allowed her time to put her family first.

So much for that plan.

"As long as you're happy, we're happy," his mother said.

Sam hoped she really meant it. Even though they gave no indication that Sam was disappointing them, he couldn't help but feel that he'd let them down. That he had let *himself* down.

Even worse, was he letting his child down?

What had happened was an accident, but ultimately the person who would pay for it would be the baby. The baby would be the one relentlessly dogged by the press. And being a royal, the stigma of illegitimacy could potentially follow him or her for life. Was it fair to put the baby through that for his own selfish needs?

It was certainly something to consider.

He had just arrived home later that evening when he got a call on his cell phone from Prince Christian's assistant, with a message from the prince. It was odd enough that she would call at almost 10:00 p.m., but how had the prince gotten his private cell number? The prince's calls typically went through Sam's office line.

Silly question. As acting king, he probably had access to any phone number he wanted.

"His Royal Highness, Prince Christian, requests your presence in the royal family's private room at the Thomas Bay yacht club tomorrow at one-thirty," she said.

Oh did he? That was an odd setting for a business meeting. Unless it had nothing to do with business. "And the nature of this meeting?" he asked her.

"A private matter."

Well, so much for believing that this would stay between Sam and Anne. He should have anticipated this. Prince Christian probably considered it his obligation to watch his sister's back. That didn't mean Sam would let him intimidate or boss him around.

"Tell the prince that I would be happy to meet him at three."

There was a brief pause, as though the idea of someone actually refusing an invitation from the prince was beyond her realm of comprehension. Finally she said, "Could you hold, please?"

"Of course."

She was off the line for several minutes, then came back on and said, "Three will be fine. The prince asks that you please keep this meeting to yourself, as it is a sensitive matter."

This suggested to Sam that Anne probably had no idea a meeting was being arranged and the prince preferred it to stay that way. He didn't doubt that the prince would try to persuade him to marry Anne. Truth be told, if Sam had a sister in a similar situation, he might do the same thing.

But this was the twenty-first century and people had children out of wedlock all the time. On occasion, even royalty. Prince Christian's wife, Princess Melissa of their sister country, Morgan Isle, was an illegitimate heir. In fact, with two illegitimate heirs, and a former king who reputedly lacked the ability or desire to keep his fly zipped, the royal family of Morgan Isle was positively brimming with scandal. By comparison the royal family of Thomas Isle were saints. Would a little scandal be so terrible?

But was it fair to the baby, who had no choice in the matter? Wasn't it a father's responsibility to protect his child?

But at what cost?

Sam slept fitfully that night and had trouble concentrating at work the next day. It was almost a relief to leave the office early, even though he doubted his meeting with the prince would be a pleasant exchange.

He arrived five minutes ahead of time, and the prince was already there, sitting in a leather armchair beside a bay of windows that overlooked the marina. He rose to greet Sam.

"Your Highness." Sam bowed his head then accepted Prince Christian's hand for a firm shake.

"I'm so glad you accepted my invitation," he said.

The Prince requests your presence sounded more like an order than an invitation. "I wasn't aware it was optional."

"I'm sorry if you were given that impression. I just thought it would be appropriate, in light of the situation, if we had a friendly chat."

Friendly? Sam doubted that.

The Prince gestured to the chair opposite him. "Please have a seat. Would you like a drink?"

A few too many glasses of champagne had gotten Sam into this mess. Had he been sober, he probably never would have approached the princess, much less danced with her. "Nothing for me, thanks."

They both sat.

"No disrespect intended, but if the *situation* you're referring to somehow involves my being the father of your sister's child, we have nothing to discuss, Your Highness."

His blunt statement seemed to surprise the prince. "Is that so?"

"It is."

"I'm afraid I disagree."

"This is between me and Anne."

"No one wishes that were the case more than I. Unfortunately, what Anne does affects our entire family. I had hoped you would do the right thing, but I understand that's not the case."

"Of course I'll do the right thing. But I'll do what *I* feel is the right thing."

"And may I ask what your idea of the right thing is?"

"As I said, that is between me and the mother of my child."

His expression darkened. He obviously didn't like that Sam wasn't falling into line. But Sam would be damned if he was going to let the prince, or any member of the royal family, walk all over him.

Prince Christian leaned forward slightly. "I won't see my sister's reputation, not to mention that of her child, decimated, because you couldn't keep out of her knickers."

What was that phrase the Americans used? It takes two to tango? "If blaming me for this situation makes you sleep better, I can live with that."

"You're being unreasonable."

"On the contrary, I'm being very reasonable. I'm considering your sister's privacy."

"This concerns more people than just you and Anne. You know that our father isn't well. A scandal like this is more than his heart could take."

So now not only was Sam decimating reputations, but he was essentially killing the king? "I'm sorry to hear that, but I'm still not talking to you."

"I could make your life unpleasant," Prince Christian said ominously. "If I feel that you're disrespecting my sister's name, I will lash out at you in any way I see fit."

So much for their *friendly* chat. He couldn't say he was surprised.

Sam shrugged. "Knock yourself out, Your Highness. I'm still not discussing my and Anne's private matters with you."

For a long moment Prince Christian just stared at him, and Sam braced himself for the fireworks. But instead of exploding with anger, the prince shook his head and laughed. "Christ, Baldwin, you've got a pair."

"I just don't respond well to threats or ultimatums."

"And I don't like giving them. But I have an obligation to look out for my family. The truth is, if it weren't for my father's fragile state, we wouldn't be having this conversation. He's in extremely poor health and it would make him very happy to see his oldest daughter married before she has a child."

He found what Prince Christian was doing utterly annoying, but in a way Sam actually felt sorry for him. "I'm truly sorry to hear that your father isn't well. I hold him in the highest regard."

"And I sympathize with your situation, Sam. I honestly do. It's common knowledge that you intend to follow in your father's footsteps and I believe you have the fortitude to pull it off. But marrying my sister would make that impossible. For what it's worth, you've built a reputation as one hell of a foreign affairs advisor. If there *were* a marriage, you would be offered a powerful and influential position within the monarchy."

After serving in, and being around, government for most of his life, the idea of taking a position with the monarchy was troubling to say the least. Not that they weren't on the same side when it came to serving the people of the country. But in Sam's eyes it had always been something of an "us against them" scenario.

Not to mention that, while he enjoyed foreign affairs, he had set his sights higher.

"Have you given any thought to how difficult it could be for your child, being illegitimate?"

"That's *all* I've been thinking about." And the more he thought about it, the more he came to realize that marrying Anne might be the wisest course of action. They may not have planned this pregnancy, but it had happened, and from now on he would have to put the welfare of his child above all else. Including his political ambitions.

"What's it like?" Sam asked. "Being a father?"

The prince smiled, his affection for his children undeniably clear. "It's exhilarating and terrifying and more rewarding than anything I've ever done. Ever *imagined*. I have these three perfect little human beings who are completely helpless and depend on me and their mother for everything they need to survive. It can be overwhelming."

"And if someone gave you a choice? Give up the throne or your children would live a life of disgrace and shame."

"No question. My children come first."

As it should be.

"You know that my wife was born out of wedlock," the prince said.

Sam nodded.

"She didn't find out that she was a royal until she was in her thirties, but it was *still* extremely difficult for her. To lay that on a child? As if life as a royal isn't tough enough already. Kids need stability, and consistency."

Things that would be much harder to give a child who

was being bounced back and forth between two parents, two households, all while being under the microscope of the press.

Sam had grown up in an ideal situation and had always hoped to provide the same for his own children. Didn't his child deserve that?

He had gone from flirting with the idea of marrying Anne to seriously considering it. And now, after talking to the prince, there seemed to be little question in his mind.

He could give it more thought, mull it around in his head for a while just to be sure, but he knew deep down the decision was already made.

He was going to marry the princess.

Four

Sam's home was not at all what Anne had expected.

She'd pictured a modern-style mansion or a seaside condo with every amenity a wealthy bachelor could want. Instead, as her driver pulled up the long gravel drive, what she got was a scene straight out of *Hansel and Gretel*.

Sam lived in a quaint cottage tucked deep in the forest and nestled under a canopy of towering pines and lazy oaks so dense only dappled sunshine dotted its sagging roof. It was quiet, and secluded, and utterly charming. Not to mention a security *nightmare*.

"Maybe we should have had dinner at the palace," she told her bodyguard, Gunter, who sat in the front seat beside her driver.

"Is no problem," he replied in a thick Russian accent. He checked his reflection in the side mirror, running a hand through his blond brush cut. Preening, she thought with a quiet smile. Physically Gunter bore a striking resemblance to Arnold Schwarzenegger in his early *Terminator* days, with a face that, Anne hated to admit, was far prettier than her own. Women swooned in his presence, never suspecting that a man so ridiculously masculine and tough lived with a cat called Toodles and a life partner named David. He had a killer fashion sense and was more intuitive than most women she knew. In fact, he had guessed that she might be pregnant before anyone in her family had even noticed. She had been in serious denial and Gunter showed up for duty with a pregnancy test.

"Is good you should know, yes?" he'd said, then he'd sat on her bed waiting while she took the test, then listened to her vent after it came back positive.

He was also ex-KGB and could snap a man's neck like a twig without breaking a sweat.

The car rolled to a stop and Gunter got out to open her door.

"I do sweep," he said, as he helped her out.

"He's the father of my child. Is that really necessary?"

Gunter just gave her one of those looks and she knew it wasn't even worth arguing. She blew out an exasperated breath for good measure and in her best annoyed tone said, *"Fine."*

The door to the cottage opened as they started up the walk and there stood Sam, looking too adorable for words, wearing dark blue slacks and a sky-blue button-up shirt with the sleeves rolled to the elbows.

He smiled, both dimples showing, and she caught herself hoping that the baby looked just like him.

Out of the corner of her eye she noticed Gunter's brows lift, almost imperceptibly, and she could swear she heard him say, *Nice,* under his breath.

Up until that instant she had only been a little nervous about seeing Sam, but suddenly her heart was going berserk in her chest and her hands were trembling.

"Hi," she said as she stepped up to the tiny, covered porch complete with a rickety rocking chair and a terra-cotta pot overflowing with yellow and purple petunias.

Sam leaned casually in the doorway, the sweet smile not budging an inch, taking in her taupe cotton skirt and yellow silk sleeveless blouse. It was the most cheerful outfit she could dredge up that still fit. Only lately had she realized just how dark and dreary her wardrobe had become over the past few years. She swore that when she got around to buying maternity clothes they would be in only bright and cheerful colors. She was turning over a new leaf so she could be someone her baby would respect and be proud of. The way she respected her own mother.

Sam's eyes traveled very unplatonically down her body then back up again, clearly liking what they saw. "You look beautiful."

"Thank you. You look nice, too." Talk about swooning. Being close to him did funny things to her head. Neurons misfired and wires crossed, creating total and utter chaos.

You're only here to talk about the baby, she reminded herself, *not to indulge your ridiculous crush.*

Beside her Gunter softly cleared his throat. Right. The sweep.

"Would you mind terribly if Gunter did a quick security check of the house?" Anne asked Sam.

It was the kind of request that might insult some people, but Sam just shrugged, gestured inside and said, "Have at it, Gunter."

Gunter pinned her with a look that said, *Don't move,* but she knew the drill.

"Wouldn't want to meet him in a dark alley," Sam said, after he disappeared inside. "Gunter. German, right?"

"On his mother's side, but he was raised in Moscow." Anne peered past him into the cottage. It was just as quaint and old-fashioned as the exterior, with older but comfortable-looking furniture and more knickknacks that even Gunter would deem appropriate for a man. And it smelled a little like...old people.

"Your house is lovely," she said. "Not at all what I expected."

"Needless to say, I'm exceedingly secure in my masculinity."

"I guess so."

He laughed. "I'm sorry but no man is that secure. The truth is, it's my grandmother's place."

Which explained the geriatric bouquet. "You live with her?"

"Only in spirit. She passed away three years ago."

"Oh, I'm so sorry."

"I'm just staying here temporarily. While my place is being worked on."

"You're remodeling?"

"You could say that, although not by choice. I've had a leak in the roof for a while, but when my bedroom and kitchen ceilings started to droop, I decided it was time to finally do something about it. But then I figured, since I would be gone anyway, it only made sense to update the kitchen while I was at it. So, three days' worth of work turned into more like three weeks." He gestured inside. "Can I give you the tour?"

"I can't, not until I get the all clear."

"Right," he said. "Just in case I have an assassin hiding under the davenport."

"I know, it's ridiculous."

His expression turned serious. "Not at all," he said, then he reached out and placed a hand over her baby bump. The gesture was so surprising, so unexpected, that her knees went weak. His eyes locked on hers, clear and intense, and his mouth was close. Too close. "Not if it keeps you and Sam Junior safe."

Hadn't they agreed that it would be prudent to keep a safe physical distance? That when they got too close they— Wait, what did he say? "Sam who?"

He grinned and gave her belly a gentle pat before he moved his hand away. "Sam Junior."

"So you think it's a boy?"

"That's the beauty of it. It works for a boy or a girl. Samuel or Samantha. Either way we call it Sam."

She folded her arms across her chest. "It would seem you have it all figured out."

He pinned his eyes on her, his gaze so intense she swore she could feel it straight through to her bones. "I'm a man who knows what he wants, Your Highness."

His eyes said he wanted her, but she knew he was

probably only teasing. But if Gunter hadn't reappeared at that very second, she might have melted into a puddle on the doorstep.

"Is all clear," Gunter said, stepping onto the porch and gesturing her in. As Sam closed the door, Anne knew that Gunter would stand on the porch, in a military stance, unmoving until it was time to leave.

"Ready for that tour?" Sam asked and she nodded. Although, honestly, there really wasn't that much to see. The front room had just enough space for a couch, glider and a rickety television stand with a TV that was probably older than her. The kitchen was small but functional, with appliances that dated back to the dark ages. But if the flame under the pot on the stove, and the hum of refrigerator, were any indication, they were both still working. The loo was also tiny, with an antique sink and commode and an antique claw-foot tub.

Next he took her into the bedrooms. The smaller of the two was being used as an office and the larger was where Sam slept. As they stood in the doorway, Anne couldn't help thinking that the last time they had been in a bedroom together they had both been out of their brains with lust for each other. It seemed like so long ago, yet she recalled every instant, every detail in Technicolor clarity.

"Sorry it's a bit of a mess," he said.

The bed was mussed and there were clothes piled over a chair in the corner. The entire house had something of a cluttered but cozy feel. And though the entire square footage was less that her sleeping chamber at the castle, she felt instantly at home there.

"I was under the impression your family had money,"

she said, feeling like a snob the instant the words were out. "I didn't mean that the way it sounded."

"That's okay," he said with a good-natured smile. "The money came from my grandfather's side. My grandmother grew up here. After her parents died, she and my grandfather would spend weekends here. After my grandfather died, she moved back permanently and stayed until she died."

"I can see why she moved back," she told him as they walked back to the kitchen. "It's really lovely."

"It's not exactly the castle."

"No, but it has loads of charm."

"And no space."

She shrugged. "It's cozy."

"And it desperately needs to be updated. Did you see that tub?"

She gazed around. "No, I wouldn't change a single thing."

He looked at her funny. "You're serious."

She smiled and nodded. She really liked it. "It's so... peaceful. The minute I walked in I felt completely at home." She could even picture herself spending time here, curled up on the couch reading a book or taking long walks through the woods. Although, until the Gingerbread Man was caught, that would never be allowed.

"I'm glad," he said, flashing her the sexy grin that made her knees go weak. "Would you like something to drink? I have soda and juice."

"Just water, please."

He got a bottle from the fridge and poured it into a

glass with a wedge of lime. As he handed it to her, their fingertips touched.

"Something smells delicious," she said.

"Chicken soup. My grandmother's recipe."

Not your typical summer food, but that was okay. "I didn't know you could cook."

He grinned and wiggled his brows. "I am a man of many talents, Your Highness."

Oh, did she know it. Although under the circumstances many of those talents were best not contemplated. "What else can you make?"

"Let's see," he said, counting off on his fingers. "I can make coffee. And toast. I can heat a pizza. Oh, and I make a mean tray of ice cubes. And did I mention the toast?"

She smiled. "So in other words, you eat out a lot?"

"Constantly. But I wanted to impress you and I figured the soup might be good since you haven't been feeling well."

It was sweet of him to consider her temperamental stomach. He was so considerate and…nice. And oh, how she wished things could be different, that they could at least try to make a go of it, try to be a family. She wanted it so much her chest ached. It was all she had been able to think about since their talk in his office the other day. He was, by definition, the man of her dreams.

But some things just weren't meant to be.

"I think maybe it was stress making me feel sick," she said. "Since I told you about the baby, I've felt much better. I'll get nauseous occasionally, but no more running to the loo. I've even gained a few pounds, which I know will make my physician happy."

"That's great." He lifted the lid off the pot of soup and gave it a stir with a wooden spoon. "The soup is ready. But would you prefer to talk first and get it out of the way? So we can relax and enjoy dinner."

"I think that would be a good idea."

He gestured to the front room. "Shall we sit on the sofa?"

She nodded and took a seat, and he sat beside her, so close that his thigh was touching hers. Was this his idea of platonic?

He had given no indication that he would be difficult, or make unreasonable demands when it came to the baby, but she still wasn't sure what to expect. Sam, in contrast, sat beside her looking completely at ease. Did the man never get his feathers ruffled? When she had fallen apart at the ball he had snapped into action and rescued her from imminent public humiliation. When she told him about the baby he had been calm and rational and even sympathetic. She had never seen, or even heard of him ever losing his temper.

She, on the other hand, always seemed to be irritated and cranky about one thing or another. She could learn a lot from Sam. Although, if he knew the truth, if he knew that this little "accident" could have easily been prevented, he might not be so understanding. She would just have to be sure that he never found out.

"Before we get started," she said, "I just want to tell you again that I appreciate how well you've taken all this. I know things could potentially get complicated at some point, with custody and financial issues, and even different parenting styles. I just want you to know that I'm going to try my best to keep things civilized. I know I don't have a reputation for being the most reasonable woman, but I'm going to try really hard."

Sam's expression was serious. "Suppose I thought of a way to make things exponentially easier on both of us. On all three of us, actually."

She couldn't imagine how, but she shrugged and said, "I'm all for easy."

"I think you should marry me."

He said it so calmly, so matter-of-factly, that the meaning of his words took several seconds to sink in. Then she was sure that she must have heard him wrong, or he was playing some cruel joke. That any second he was going to laugh and say, "Gotcha!"

"I know it's fast," he said instead. "I mean, we barely know each other. But, for the baby's sake, I really think it's the logical next move."

My God, he was *serious*. He wanted to marry her. How was that even possible when only a few days ago it supposedly hadn't been an option?

"But...you want to be prime minister."

"Yes, but that isn't what's best for the baby. I'm going to be a father. From now on, I have to put his or her best interests first."

She had a sudden, unsettling thought. "My family isn't making you do this, are they? Did they threaten you?"

"This has nothing to do with your family." He took her hand and held it between his two. "This is what I want, Annie. What I think is best for everyone. We have to at least try, for the baby's sake."

She was thrilled to the center of her being…and drowning in a churning sea of guilt. If she had just acted responsibly, if she hadn't lied about being protected, they wouldn't be in this situation. He wouldn't be forced to give up everything that he had worked so hard for.

What if it was a decision he regretted someday and he grew to resent her and the baby? But what if he didn't? What if they fell in love and lived a long and happy life together?

She folded her other hand over his two. "Sam, are you *sure* about this? Because once we're married, that's it. A divorce can only be granted with the consent of the king."

"Let's try this another way," he said, then he dropped down on one knee in front of her and produced a diamond ring from his pants pocket.

She could hardly believe that this was really happening. It was a real, honest-to-goodness proposal.

He took her hand, looked deep in her eyes. "Will you marry me, Annie?"

There was only one answer she could give him. "Of course I'll marry you, Sam."

Grinning, he slid the ring on her finger. It was fashioned from white gold with a round cut diamond deeply set and surrounded by smaller stones. Despite its shine it was clearly an antique, not to mention exquisitely beautiful.

"Oh, Sam, it's amazing."

"It was my great-grandmother's," he said.

"We must have the same size finger," she said, turning her hand to watch it sparkle. "It's a perfect fit."

"I had it sized."

"But how did you know what size to make it?"

"Princess Louisa."

"You asked my sister?"

"Is that okay?"

"Of course. I just can't believe she didn't say anything. She's horrible at keeping secrets."

"I guess she wanted our moment to be special."

"It is." She threw her arms around his neck and hugged him and he hugged her back just as hard. It felt so good to hold him, to be close to him. It felt like... coming home. And she realized, she was truly happy. The happiest she had been in a long, *long* time. Maybe ever.

It was astonishing how, out of such a complicated situation, something so fantastic could arise. Ideally, he would have slipped sentiments of love somewhere between the rationale, but she was sure that would come later. Not that she believed it would be all smooth sailing. She knew that marriages took work and this one would be no exception. But they seemed to be off to a fairly good start under the circumstances.

"I know he's not well, but if at all possible, I'd like to be there when you tell the king and queen," Sam said. "I'd like to do this by the book and have the chance to ask for your hand."

His words made her practically burst with joy, because he would be giving her father something he had always looked forward to. "We'll go to them tomorrow," she said, already excited at the prospect, because she knew that her parents would be thrilled for her. Even if Sam was a politician. And they would be so excited about the baby.

"Needless to say, we should have the wedding soon," he said. "I was thinking next week."

That was really soon, but he was right. The sooner the better. It would have to be a small ceremony, if for no other reason than her father's health. It was the reason Louisa had kept her own wedding small and intimate, despite having always dreamed of a huge, traditional affair.

Not one to like being in the spotlight, Anne would be quite content with small and simple. That didn't mean there weren't a million things to do to prepare.

Her mind was suddenly flooded with all the plans they had to make and the short amount of time they had to make them. Where would they have the ceremony and who would they invite? And would the king be well enough to walk her down the aisle? And what about a honeymoon? Where would they—

That thought brought her mind to a screeching halt.

What about the honeymoon? And even more important, the *wedding night?*

Suddenly she was ultra-aware of Sam's arms around her, his body pressed against hers. The heat of his palms on her back and the spicy scent of his aftershave.

Suddenly her heart was beating so hard and fast she was sure Sam must have felt it through her clothes and skin. And all she could think about was getting him naked again. Touching him and kissing him all over. He must have been able to read her mind, because his breath hitched and his arms tightened around her.

"So, I guess this means that we don't have to keep our relationship platonic any longer," she said.

"Funny," he said. "But I was just thinking the exact same thing."

Thank God. Because frankly, a marriage without sex would be bloody awful.

She turned her face into the crook of his neck and kissed the side of his throat, could feel the heavy thump-thump of his pulse against her lips, and knew that he was just as aroused as she was. "We could make love right now if we wanted to."

"We could," he agreed, groaning when she nipped him with her teeth. She felt as though she wanted to eat him alive. Swallow him whole. She lifted her head, and the second she did he captured her lips with his own, but instead of the slick, ravenous kiss she was expecting, *hoping* for even, his lips rubbed softly, almost sweetly over hers. He kissed her chin and her throat, working his way down.

"Take me into your bedroom," she urged, sliding her hands up to tangle in the curls at his nape, feeling so hot she could burst into flames. "Right now."

"God knows I want you," he said, brushing his lips over her collarbone. "I've wanted you since that night. It's all I've been able to think about."

"You can have me. Right now."

He trailed his way back up to her mouth and whispered against her lips, "Or we could wait until we're married."

She groaned her disappointment. She wasn't even sure she *could* wait. "I feel as though I might go out of my mind if I can't have you right now."

"All the more reason to wait," he said, sounding far

too rational. "Think of how special it would be on our wedding night."

She opened her eyes to look at him and smiled. "Isn't that supposed to be *my* line?"

He grinned. "Poke fun all you want, but you know I'm right."

Yes, he was right. Not that anything about their relationship up to this point could be called conventional. She might have worried that he just didn't want her, and was trying to let her down gently, but the tent in his pants and the color in his cheeks said he was just as aroused as she was.

"Is that really what you want?"

He took her hands from around his neck and held them, his expression earnest. "I think we should wait."

It was clear that this wasn't an easy decision for him to make, and if she pushed the issue he would probably cave and make passionate love to her all night long. She didn't really understand why this was so important to him, but it clearly was. Besides, what was a few more days?

She would respect his wishes and wait for her wedding night, she decided grudgingly. But that didn't mean she had to like it.

Five

Anne was barely home for five minutes that evening when Louisa knocked on her bedroom door. It was nearly eleven—well past Louisa and Garrett's usual bedtime. Garrett had taken over management of all the royal family's vast farmlands so their brother Aaron could go to medical school, so he rose well before sunrise every morning. Not to mention that Louisa and Garrett were still newlyweds. They were constantly holding hands and touching. Sharing secret smiles and longing glances, as though they couldn't wait to be alone.

Anne would even admit to being jealous a time or two. But soon it would be her turn.

"You're up late," Anne said, pretending she had no idea why Louisa was so eager to speak to her, keeping her hand casually behind her, so she wouldn't see the ring.

"I just wondered how your date went," Louisa said, stepping into the room and closing the door behind her.

"Technically it wasn't a date," Anne said, walking to the bed and sitting down with her hands under her thighs. "We just had things to discuss."

Louisa sat beside her. "What did you talk about?"

"The baby mostly."

"That's it?" Louisa hedged.

"Pretty much," she said, then added casually, "Oh, and he asked me to marry him."

Louisa squealed so loudly Anne was sure the entire castle heard her. "Oh my God! Congratulations! What did you say?"

She shrugged. "I told him I would think about it."

Louisa gasped in horror, looking as though she wanted to throttle her. "You didn't!"

"Of course not." She grinned and pulled her hand from under her leg, flashing Louisa the ring. "I said yes."

Louisa threw her arms around Anne and hugged her. "I am so happy for you, Annie. You and Sam are going to be perfect together."

"I really hope so," Anne said.

Louisa held her at arm's length. "You will. If you believe it, it'll happen."

She wished that were true, that it were that easy. "I just keep thinking about you and Aaron and Chris. You all found the perfect person for you—you're all so happy."

"And you will be, too."

"It just seems as though every family has at least

one person who goes through life always ruining relationships. What if I'm that person? I've always been so negative. What if I don't deserve to be happy?"

"After all we've been through with our father, don't you think we *all* deserve some happiness? Besides, nothing is predetermined. Your life is what you make of it."

"That's what I'm worried about. Up until now, I've made a mess of it. Especially my love life."

"That was just bad luck. You just happened to meet a string of jerks. But anyone who knows Sam will tell you he's a great guy. And he'll be a fantastic husband and father."

Anne didn't doubt that at all. She never would have accepted his proposal otherwise. It was herself she was worried about. For the first time in her life she had a real shot at happiness—and she was terrified that she would find a way to screw it up.

"I'm sure you're right," she told Louisa.

"Of course I am," she said, as if there was never a doubt. Her relentless optimism never ceased to amaze Anne.

After Louisa went back to her room, Anne changed into her softest pajamas and crawled into bed, but her mind was still moving a million miles an hour and she was practically bursting with excitement. Thinking that a cup of tea might soothe her nerves, she climbed out of bed and put on her robe. The halls of the castle were silent but for the muffled wail of a baby crying from Chris and Melissa's room. Five months from now Anne could look forward to the same. She *and* Sam, she reminded herself with a smile.

She expected the kitchen to be empty and was surprised, when she switched on the light, to find their butler, Geoffrey, sitting at the butcher-block table. He squinted at the sudden bright light.

"I'm sorry," Anne said. "I didn't mean to startle you."

"No need to apologize," he said. His jacket was draped over the back of his chair and his tie hung loose around his neck. In front of him sat a bottle of scotch and a half-full highball glass. "What brings you down here at this late hour, Your Highness?"

"Couldn't sleep. I thought I would make some tea."

"You should have called down," he scolded. "I'd have brought it to you."

"I didn't want to bother you."

He rose and gestured to an empty chair. "Sit. I'll make it for you."

Because this was Geoffrey's domain, and he could be a little territorial, she did as he asked. She gestured to his drink and said, "Rough day?"

"Worse than some, better than others." He put the kettle on to boil. "How about you?"

"Actually, I had a very good day."

He pulled a cup down from the cupboard and dropped a tea bag in. "Would that have something to do with a certain young man and that ring on your finger?"

"It might." She should have realized he would notice the ring. Geoffrey didn't miss a thing. He may have been getting up in years, but he was still sharp as a tack. He had been with the family since before she was born and in some ways she had come to think of him as a second father. As far as she knew he had no family of his own, no one to care for him if he ever became incapacitated. But after so many years of loyal service, he would always have a place at the castle with the royal family.

"I suppose you heard about the baby."

"I might have," he said cryptically, but knowing him, he'd probably suspected all along.

"Are you disappointed in me?"

"If you had murdered someone, I would have been disappointed in you. A child is a blessing."

"Yes, but I know you have...*traditional* values."

He poured boiling water into her cup then set it on the table in front of her. "Then I suppose you'll be surprised to learn that I was once in a similar situation."

Surprised? For a moment she was too stunned to even respond. She never knew him to have a girlfriend, much less a pregnant one. He'd never spoken of any family. "I—I had no idea."

He sat across from her. "It was many years ago. Before I came to work here."

"You have a child?"

He nodded. "His name is Richard."

"Why didn't you ever say anything?"

He shrugged, swirling the amber liquid in his glass. "It isn't something I like to talk about."

"Do you see him?"

He shook his head, looking remorseful. "Not for many years."

"What happened?"

He downed the last of his drink then poured himself another. She wondered if the alcohol was responsible for his sudden loose tongue. He looked so sad. And when had he gotten so old? It was as though the lines on his face had appeared overnight. Or maybe she just hadn't wanted to see them.

"His mother was a cook for my previous employer," he told her. "We had an affair and she became pregnant. I did the responsible thing and married her, but it didn't take long to realize that we were completely incompatible. We stayed together for two years, then finally divorced. But working together was unpleasant for both of us, so we decided it would be best if I left and found a new job. That was when I came to work here."

"When did you stop seeing your son?"

"When he was six his mother remarried. At first I was jealous, but this man was good to Richard. He treated him like his own son. A year later he was offered a position in England. I objected at first, but my ex pointed out what was obvious. I didn't have time for my son and his stepfather did. She convinced me that it would be best if I let him go."

"That must have been devastating for you."

"It was the hardest thing I've ever done. I tried to keep in touch with phone calls and letters, but we drifted apart. I think he just didn't need me any longer."

He looked so sad that tears burned the corners of Anne's eyes. She reached out and placed a hand on top of his. Learning this was such a shock. Had she never considered that he had a life that she knew nothing about? Had she believed his life hadn't really begun until he'd come to work for them? That his world was so small and insignificant? "I'm so sorry, Geoffrey."

Even his eyes looked a bit misty. "I was saddened,

but by then I had you and your siblings to chase around. Only now I fear I made a terrible mistake by letting him go."

He looked so sad it made her want to hug him. "You did what you thought was best. And that doesn't mean you can't try to contact him now. Do you have any idea where he lives? What he does for a living?"

"The last time I talked to his mother, he was serving as a Royal Marine Commando."

"Goodness! That's impressive."

"She bragged that he was some sort of computer genius. But that was more than ten years ago."

"You could at least try to look him up."

He rubbed his thumb around the rim of his glass. "What if I do, and I don't like what I find?"

She wondered why he would think a thing like that. He should at least try to find him.

Geoffrey swallowed the last of his drink and looked at his watch. "It's nearly midnight. I should turn in. And so should you, young lady."

She smiled. He hadn't called her that in years. "Yes, sir."

As he walked past her to his quarters behind the kitchen he patted her shoulder. She was struck by how his capable hands were beginning to look wrinkled and bony.

She looked down and realized she hadn't taken a single sip of her tea, and now it had gone cold.

The king had been out of the public eye for such a long period of time that Sam was genuinely stunned when he saw him the following afternoon. Though he knew the king was in ill health, never had he expected him to look so pale and fragile. Practically swimming in too-large flannel pajamas and a bulky robe—that Sam was sure had probably fit him at one time—the king looked painfully thin and small. A mere shell of the larger-than-life figure he used to be. And it was obvious that the months of sitting at his side had visibly taken their toll on Anne's mother. The queen looked utterly exhausted and beaten down. Her features, once bright and youthful, now looked drawn and tired, as though she had aged a decade in only months.

But the grief they suffered did nothing to dampen their joy when Sam announced his intention to marry Anne and asked them for her hand. Though the king may have been physically fragile, when it came to his mental faculties, he was clearly all there. "I had hoped you would do the right thing, Sam," the king told him. "For my grandchild's sake."

"Of course you'll want to have the wedding soon," the queen told Anne. "Before you're really showing."

For a moment Sam felt slighted, since they had agreed to tell her parents together, then he glanced over at Anne, saw her stunned expression, and realized that she hadn't said a word.

So much for the news being too much for the king's heart to take, Sam thought wryly. His children obviously underestimated him.

"I'm going to kill Louisa!" Anne growled, looking as though she would do just that. "Or was it Chris who snitched?"

Sam folded his arms across his chest and casually covered his mouth to hide a grin. So this was the feisty side of Anne he had heard so much about. He kind of liked it.

"No one said a word," the queen assured her. "They didn't have to. I know my daughter."

"And though I may be an invalid," the king added, shooting a meaningful look Sam's way, "I stay well-informed as to what goes on in my castle."

Things like Sam sneaking out of his daughter's bedroom in the wee hours of the morning.

The king chuckled weakly. "Don't look so chastened. I was a young man once, too, you know." He looked over at his wife and smiled. "And there was a time when I did my fair share of sneaking around."

The queen reached over and took his hand and they shared a smile. It was clear that despite all they had been through, or maybe because of it, they were still deeply in love. Sam hoped that someday it would be like that for him and Anne.

"Why didn't you say anything?" Anne asked, looking genuinely distressed.

"Sweetheart," her mother said. "You've always been one to take your time and work things through. I assumed that when you were ready for us to know, you would tell us. And if you needed my guidance, you would have asked for it."

"You're not upset?" Anne asked, looking a bit like a naughty child who feared a sound lashing for misbehaving.

"Are you happy?" the king asked her.

She looked over at Sam and smiled. "I am. Very happy."

"Then what do I have to be upset about?"

"Well, the baby—"

"Is a blessing," the queen said.

Their casual attitude toward the situation surprised Sam, but then, after all they had been through, and knowing the king was living on borrowed time, what point would there be to make a huge fuss and create hard feelings?

Sam had always respected the king, but never so much as he did now. And despite what his father believed about them thinking *differently,* they seemed to be exceptionally well grounded in reality.

"I assume that you intend to live here, at the castle," the king said.

Anne glanced nervously his way. Where they would live hadn't yet come up, but Sam knew what was expected. "Of course, Your Highness."

"And of course you will work for the royal family."

Sam nodded. "I would be honored."

"Have you thought about what colors you would like for your wedding?" the queen asked Anne.

"Yellow, I think," Anne said, and she and her mother drifted off to discuss wedding plans while Sam spoke to the king about his future position in the monarchy. He assured Sam that his talents would not be wasted, nor would they go unrewarded. Sam's inheritance guaranteed him a financially sound future, so salary wasn't an issue, but he was happy to know they valued his service. And relieved that under the circumstances, this entire situation was running as smoothly as a well-oiled machine.

So well that, were he not such a positive thinker, he might be waiting for the other shoe to fall.

* * *

The following Friday, with only the royal family, Sam's parents and a few close friends in attendance, Sam and Anne were wed in a small, private ceremony in the garden on the palace grounds. The weather couldn't have been more ideal. Sunny and clear with a temperature in the low seventies.

Louisa was the matron of honor and Sam's older brother, Adam, flew in from England to be his best man. A musician and composer, Adam couldn't have been less interested in politics, yet the artist in him understood Sam's lifelong passion, and his desire to follow in their father's footsteps.

"You're sure you want to do this?" he asked Sam just before the ceremony was about to begin. "If you're doing this to salvage the princess's reputation—"

"I'm doing this because my child deserves to have parents who are married."

"A one-night fling does not make for a lasting relationship, Sam. You barely know her. If the royal family is forcing you into this—"

"This is my choice, and mine alone."

Adam shook his head, as though Sam were a lost cause. Then he grinned and said, "My baby brother, a *duke*. Who would have thought?"

Sam appreciated his brother's concern, that after all these years Adam was still looking out for him. But Sam had already put the political chapter of his life behind him. He'd spent the last two days cleaning out his office at work since, as of that morning, he had been given the official title of duke and by law could no longer serve in government. His secretary, Grace, had tearfully said goodbye, telling him what an exceptional boss he'd been and how she would miss him. She said she was proud of him.

"I know I haven't been the most efficient secretary and I appreciate your patience with me."

Of course he felt guilty as hell for all the times he'd gotten frustrated and snapped at her or regarded her impatiently.

After he and Anne returned from their honeymoon Sam would take up his new position with the monarchy. He couldn't say he was thrilled by the prospect, but he was trying to keep an open mind and a positive attitude. At least they didn't try to force him into their agricultural business. A farmer, he was not. He didn't know the first thing about managing farmland and raising crops. Nor did he have any inclination to learn.

His new goal was to surpass his new position as foreign affairs director and when Chris officially became king, become his right hand.

The music began, and Sam looked up to see Anne and her father taking their places. She wore a crème-colored floor-length dress with layers of soft silk ruffles. But even that did little to disguise the fact that she was pregnant. Not that everyone there didn't already know. He would swear that since she had come to see him last week her tummy had nearly doubled in size. But as far as he was concerned it only made her look more ravishing.

Her hair was piled up on her head in loose curls with soft wisps trailing down to frame her face. And of course she wore a jewel-encrusted tiara.

Everyone stood to receive her, and Sam watched,

mesmerized as she walked slowly toward him, looking radiant. She seemed to glow from the inside out with happiness.

It was obvious, the way the king clung to her arm as he walked her down the short path, that it was taking every bit of strength he could muster to make the short trip. But he did it with grace and dignity.

Here we go, Sam thought, as the king linked his and Anne's hands together. It was the end of life as he once knew it. But as they spoke their vows and exchanged rings, instead of feeling cornered or trapped, he felt a deep sense of calm. He took that as a sign that he truly was doing the right thing. Maybe not just for their child, but for the two of them, as well.

Following the ceremony, drinks and hors d'oeuvres were served under a tent on the castle grounds. After a bit of mingling, Sam stood by the bar, watching his new wife. She was chatting with his brother and Adam seemed quite taken with her. Under the circumstances Sam might have expected some tension between their families, but everyone seemed to get along just fine. Almost *too* well.

Price Christian stepped up to the bar to get a drink, and told Sam, "Nice wedding."

Sam nodded. "It was."

He got his drink then turned to stand beside Sam. "I've never seen my sister so happy."

She did look happy. And Sam was glad that his family had the chance to see this side of her, the one so unlike what they had read in the press and heard about through the rumor mill. He liked to think of this Anne as *his*

Anne, the real woman inside, whom he had rescued from an existence of negativity and despair.

They had done a lot of talking this week in preparation for their wedding and she'd opened up about some of the past men in her life. The ones who had used and betrayed her. After all she had been through, it was a wonder she hadn't lost her ability to trust entirely.

She saw him watching her and flashed him a smile.

"Your sister deserves to be happy," Sam told the prince.

"I think so, too." Then he added with a wry grin, "And if you ever do hurt her, I'll have to hurt you back."

Sam was quite sure, despite the prince's smile, it was said only partly in jest. "I'll keep that in mind, Your Highness."

From across the tent a baby's cry split the quiet murmur of conversation and they both turned to see Princess Melissa wrestling with two squirming bundles.

"I guess that's my cue," the prince said. He started to walk away, then stopped and said, "By the way, since we're family now, you can drop the 'Your Highness' thing and just call me Chris."

"After all these years of addressing you formally, that might take some getting used to."

"Tell me about it," Chris said with a grin before he walked off to rescue his wife.

Sam felt a hand on his arm and turned to see Anne standing there.

She slipped her arm through his and tucked herself

close to his side and said excitedly, "Can you believe it, Sam? We're *married*."

"Strange, isn't it?"

"Do you think it's odd that I'm so happy?"

"Not at all." He leaned down to brush a kiss across her lips. "I would be worried if you weren't."

"How soon do you think we can sneak out of here? I'm guessing that we could squeeze in some alone time before we leave for our honeymoon."

He was about to say, *as soon as possible,* when an explosion pierced his ears and shook the ground beneath his feet. Startled cries from the guests followed and Anne screeched in surprise. Sam instinctively shielded her with his body and looked in the direction of the sound as a ball of fire and smoke billowed up from the north side of the castle. At first he could hardly believe what he was seeing—his first instinct was to get Anne somewhere safe as quickly as possible—but before he had an instant to act, the entire area was crawling with security.

"What the bloody hell is going on?" Anne demanded, shoving past him to see, and when she saw the flames and smoke darkening the clear blue afternoon sky, the color drained from her face.

Security was already rounding everyone up and guiding them in the opposite direction, away from the blast.

"It's him," Anne said, looking more angry than afraid, watching as acrid smoke began to blow in their direction. "The Gingerbread Man did this."

Threatening e-mails and occasional pranks were an

annoyance, but this was a serious escalation. He was obviously out of control. If it was even him. "For all we know it could be an accident," he told her.

"No," she said firmly. "It's him. And this time he's gone too far."

Six

As Anne had suspected, the explosion had been deliberate.

The device had been hidden in the undercarriage of a car that belonged to Sam's aunt and uncle. The police bomb squad still had investigating to do, but as far as they could tell, the bomb had been detonated remotely.

Four other cars had been damaged in the blast and the castle garage had taken a serious hit. Four of the five doors would need to be replaced and the facade would require repair. Thankfully, no people had been seriously hurt. He'd had the decency to do it when there weren't a lot of people close by. Or maybe that had just been dumb luck. A few maintenance people walked away with mild abrasions and first-degree burns, but it could have been so much worse.

Sam's poor aunt and uncle, whose car had been sabotaged, were beside themselves with guilt. They felt responsible, even though Anne and her siblings assured them repeatedly that they were in no way being blamed. There was only one person responsible for this.

The Gingerbread Man.

They knew this for a fact now because shortly after the explosion he'd sent an e-mail to Anne via the security office.

Sorry I couldn't make it to your wedding.
Heard it was a blast.

"This has got to stop!" she told Chris, who sat slumped in a chair in the study, nursing a scotch. The wedding guests had all been driven home in the royal fleet—since their own cars had been casualties of the explosion—and most of the family had gone up to bed. Only she, Sam and Chris stayed behind to talk. Or in her case, castigate. She was so filled with nervous energy she hadn't stopped pacing, hadn't stopped moving in hours. "Someone could have been seriously hurt. Someone could have *died!*"

"You think I don't know that?" Chris said, looking exhausted. "We're doing all that we can. What else would you have me do?"

"You know what I think we should do," she said, and his expression went dark.

"That is *not* an option."

"What's not an option?" Sam asked from his seat on the settee. He had been so understanding about this, considering his wedding day had literally gone up in smoke. But she had warned him that being with her could potentially suck him into this mess. And so it had. She shuddered to think what would have happened if the Gingerbread Man had waited until the guests were leaving to sink the plunger. She was sure Sam had considered the same possibilities.

"She wants us to try to draw him out so we can catch him," Chris said.

"Draw him out *how?*"

"I assume by using one of us as bait."

Sam turned to look at her. "You're not serious."

"Maybe I trust our security team to do their job. Besides, no one else has had a better idea. How long are we supposed to go on like this? Living like prisoners, in fear of what he'll do next. He's obviously escalating the violence."

"Obviously," Chris snapped. He rarely lost his cool, so Anne knew that he was much more upset about this than he was letting on. "And now we know what he's capable of. He's not just some twisted stalker. He made a bomb. He's more dangerous than *any* of us anticipated."

"Okay," she acknowledged. "Maybe luring him out wouldn't be such a hot idea after all."

"I think that, in light of what happened, it would be best if you two canceled your honeymoon."

"What!" she screeched, indignation roiling up in her like a volcano. "You can't be serious."

"I'm very serious."

"But you're the one who suggested we go there, because it would be safe."

She and Sam had been invited by Chris's brother-in-law, King Phillip of Morgan Isle—the sister to Thomas Isle—to use their family hunting lodge. In fact, they should have been on a boat to the other island hours ago. If things had gone as planned, they would already be celebrating their honeymoon.

"I thought it would be the safest place for you, but—"

"Louisa went to Cabo for her honeymoon and no one gave her a hard time," Anne reminded him.

"Circumstances have changed."

"Chris, he *ruined* my wedding. I refuse to let him ruin my honeymoon, too. We'll have plenty of security there. We'll be *fine*."

He still looked hesitant.

"The location was kept so hush-hush that by the time he figures out where we are, and comes up with his next diabolical plan, we'll be back to the castle."

"All right," he finally agreed. "As long as you promise not to take any unnecessary risks."

"Of course." Did he think that she was a complete dolt? She wanted the man caught and brought to justice, but not so badly that she would endanger the life of her child.

Chris looked at Sam, who nodded and said, "We won't."

Is that how it would be now? Her family looking to her husband to keep her in line?

She realized she was clenching her fists and forced herself to relax. Getting this worked up wasn't good for her or the baby. What she needed was an outlet for all this tension and stress. And she didn't have to look far to find one.

She gazed over at Sam. Her *husband*. He was still wearing his wedding clothes but he'd shed the jacket and loosened his tie. The hair that had been combed back from his face earlier now fell forward in soft curls across his forehead. He looked too adorable for words and she couldn't wait to put her hands all over him.

Her wedding day may have been decimated, but they still had their wedding night. After four months of missing his touch, and a torturous week of waiting for this very night, she was determined to make it a memorable one.

"I'm exhausted," she announced, forcing a yawn for added effect, when in reality she was so awake she was practically buzzing. "Are you ready for bed, Sam?"

He nodded and rose from the settee.

"I'll arrange to have the boat ready for your trip to Morgan Isle at 10:00 a.m.," Chris told her.

"Thank you," she said, taking Sam's hand, leading him out of the study and up the stairs to her room. Make that *their* room. Most of Sam's clothes and toiletries had been moved in earlier that morning, which had necessitated her clearing a place in her closet for him. Sharing her space again would require some getting used to. Louisa and Anne had shared a bedroom until they were thirteen and Anne could no longer stand the frilly pink bedcovers and curtains, the childish furnishings. Furnishings Louisa had still used until a few months ago.

What Anne really hoped was that when this Gingerbread Man business was behind them, she and Sam could spend time at his grandmother's cottage. Away from her family and the confines of her title. A place where she could just be herself. A place where, unlike the castle, portraits of her relatives didn't stare accusingly from every hallway. And where she could make herself a cup of tea without feeling like an intruder in the kitchen. Where she could make love to her husband and not worry that someone on the opposite side of the wall would hear her.

Privacy. That was what she wanted. A place of her own.

"I need to apologize," Sam said.

She looked over at him. "For what?"

"Until today, I really didn't take this Gingerbread Man thing very seriously. It seemed more an annoyance than a serious threat. But when that car exploded, I swear I saw my life flash before my eyes."

She squeezed his hand. "I'm sorry I dragged you into this."

He looked at her and smiled. "I'm not. I just want you to be safe."

Which he had proven. The first minute or so after the blast was a bit of a blur, but the one thing she did remember with distinct clarity was the way he had used his own body as a shield to protect her. She could say with much certainty that in a similar situation, the men who had come before him would have ignored her entirely and saved their own asses.

And now it seemed only fair to reward him for his chivalry. Right?

They reached her room—*their* room—and the instant they were inside with the door closed, she launched herself at him. He let out a startled "Oof!" as she threw her arms around his neck and crushed her lips to his.

But it didn't take him long to recover from his surprise, before his arms went around her and he leaned in, took control of the kiss. In that single joining of their mouths, the tangling of their tongues, they seemed to unleash months of pent-up sexual frustration. She curled her fingers through his hair and sucked on his tongue, wishing she could crawl inside his skin, anything to be *closer* to him.

When they came up for air they were both breathing hard and he was wearing a slightly confused expression. "I thought you were exhausted."

"What was I supposed to say? Let's go upstairs so you can shag me silly?"

A slow smile curled his lips. "Is that what I get to do?"

"If you want to," she said, already knowing by the look in his eyes the answer was yes. She pulled the pins from her hair, shaking it loose and letting it spill down over her shoulders. His eyes raked over her and she could swear she actually felt his gaze caressing her skin.

"Unless you'd rather just go to sleep," she teased.

To answer her, he wrapped an arm around her waist, tugged her against him and kissed her. And kissed her.

And *kissed* her.

A part of her wanted to drag him to the bed, rip off his clothes, impale herself on his body and ride him to ecstasy. The other part wanted to take her time, draw out the anticipation and make this last.

She broke the kiss and backed out of his arms, wearing a come-and-get-me smile as she unzipped her dress and pulled it over her head. All she wore underneath was a beige lace bra and matching panties.

"Take it all off," he ordered, transfixed as she unhooked her bra and dropped it on the floor.

"They're bigger," she said, cupping her breasts in her palms.

"I don't care what size they are, as long as they're attached to you."

How was it that he always knew the exact right thing to say?

She gave each one a gentle squeeze, careful to avoid her nipples. They had been especially sensitive since the second month of her pregnancy. Sometimes just the brush of her pajama top made them hard and tingly, almost to the point of pain.

"The panties, too," he demanded.

She slid them down, anticipating the slow smile that curled his mouth when he realized what she was hiding—or more to the point *wasn't* hiding— underneath.

"I think I just died and went to heaven," he said.

"It was Louisa's idea," she told him, touching her fingers to the smooth skin from the recent Brazilian wax that her sister had *insisted* would drive Sam wild. If the look on his face was any indication, she was right.

"Louisa, huh?" He shook his head. "She just doesn't seem the type."

No kidding. For someone who had clung to her virginity until her engagement several months ago, Louisa seemed to know an awful lot about sex. "She said it enhances sensation."

"I guess we'll have to test that theory."

She was counting on it. She backed toward the bed and Sam watched as she pulled back the covers and draped herself across the mattress, letting her legs casually fall open. Giving him a view of the full package.

He started to walk toward her but she shook her head and said, "Uh-uh," and he stopped in his tracks. She gestured to his clothes. "Your turn to undress. Take it all off."

If there were a land speed record for disrobing, he probably broke it. And he had the most beautiful body she had ever seen. Long and lean and perfect. Simply looking at him made her feel all hot and fidgety and anxious.

"Lie down," he ordered.

She scooted over and lay back against the pillows. Sam crawled in and settled down beside her. She was so ready for him she ached, but she didn't want to rush this. She wanted to savor every second. Sam seemed content just lying there looking at her, lightly caressing the tops of her breasts, the column of her throat.

"You are so beautiful," he said, his eyes already shiny and heavy-lidded with arousal. He cupped her breasts, testing their weight in his hand, then he leaned over and licked the dark crest of one. She knew her nipples were sensitive, she just hadn't realized *how* sensitive until he nipped one with his teeth. Her body jerked violently, as though he were holding a live wire to her skin, and a strangled moan ripped from her throat.

He lifted his head, looking equal parts alarmed and intrigued. "What just happened?"

"I don't know," she said, her voice unsteady with shock and arousal. "I've never felt anything like that."

"Was it bad?"

"Not exactly. It felt…*electric*." Pleasure and pain all wrapped up in one.

"Should I stop?"

She shook her head. "Do it again."

"You're sure?"

She bit her lip and nodded. He lowered his head to try again and she grabbed his shoulders, bracing herself. But nothing could have prepared her for the assault of sensation as he sucked her nipple into his mouth. There was a tremendous, almost unbearably intense throb between her thighs, as if her breasts had somehow been hardwired directly to her womb. A moan rolled up from deep in her chest and her nails dug into his flesh. Then he did the same to the opposite side and she nearly vaulted off the bed, so far gone that she was on another planet.

Sam released her nipple and gazed down at her, looking fascinated, like a child who had just been handed a new toy. "Wow."

No kidding. This was completely crazy. He'd barely touched her and already she was hovering on the verge of an orgasm. Her body was so alive that if he so much as looked at her cross-eyed, she was going to lose it.

"If you do that again, I'll come," she warned him.

"Seriously?"

She nodded.

He looked like he wanted to, if for no other reason than to see if she really would. He even started to lean forward, then seemed to change his mind at the last second. Instead he pushed himself up, pressing her thighs apart and kneeling between them.

She thought he would enter her right away, but he leaned forward instead and licked her. Whether it was the bare skin enhancing things, or her fragile sexual state making it especially erotic, she couldn't really say. And didn't really care. All she knew was that it felt so out-of-this-world fantastic she actually forgot to breathe.

"I've been fantasizing about being with you since that night in your room," he said, pressing a kiss to her swollen belly. "I haven't been able to even look at another woman. I've only wanted you."

She threaded her fingers through his hair as he kissed and nibbled his way up her body, driving her mad. She was sure that was exactly what he intended. When he finally lowered himself on top of her, she was half out of her mind from wanting him and desperate for release.

He eased into her, one slow, steady, *deep* thrust, and a burst of electricity started deep in her core and zinged outward until only the boundaries of her skin kept it from jumping from her body to his.

His eyes locked on hers as he pulled back, then he rocked into her again, only this time she arched her hips up to meet him halfway and there were no words to describe the shocking pleasure, the sensations building inside her. It robbed her ability to think, to reason. All she could do was feel.

Every thrust drove her higher, closer to nirvana, then Sam clamped his mouth over her breast and her body finally let go. Pleasure flooded her senses in a violent rush, sinking in like a wild animal, feral and out of control.

Through a haze she heard Sam moan, heard him

say her name, felt his breath hot on her neck as his body locked and shuddered. In that instant nothing else mattered. It was just the two of them, just her and Sam against the world. Two souls twining and fusing in an irreversible bond.

She knew without a doubt that she loved him. And not just because he'd given her the best orgasm of her life. They were soul mates. She had known it the minute he'd taken her in his arms on the dance floor the night of the charity ball.

But she couldn't tell him. Not yet. The time just didn't feel right.

Sam started kissing her neck, nibbling her ears, whispering how delicious she tasted and she felt herself being dragged back under, into that deep well of desire. And before she even had a chance to catch her breath, he was making love to her all over again.

Seven

Considering it was owned by royalty, the hunting lodge on Morgan Isle was just about as stripped down and bare bones as it could be. It was a log cabin shell with a small kitchen, great room, two bathrooms—one on each floor—and four small, sparsely furnished bedrooms. Two upstairs, two down. And of course there were the obligatory stuffed dead animals all over the place.

There was no television or radio. No phone. Sam even insisted that he and Anne surrender their cell phones to Gunter, and made it clear that shy of a catastrophic disaster or urgent family matter, they were not to be disturbed. He didn't want a single thing to distract them from his primary goal. Get Anne naked and keep her that way for the next six days. And she seemed to have the same thing in mind. When he'd commented on her conspicuous lack of luggage—she'd brought only one small bag—she'd shrugged and said, "It's our honeymoon. What do I need clothes for?"

It was nice to know they were on the same page, since last night had been, by far, the hottest sex of his entire life. He'd been fantasizing about being with her for months, but the scenarios he'd created in his mind had paled in comparison to the real thing. And though he enjoyed getting off as much as the next man, nothing could have been more satisfying than watching Anne writhe and shudder in ecstasy. He'd made her come six times—*six times*—which under normal circumstances should have earned him some sort of accolade. But the truth was, he'd barely had to work at it.

He'd been with women who were difficult to please. But with Anne it didn't make a difference what position they happened to be in—if he was on top or she was, or if he took her pressed up against the shower wall, which he'd done twice. All he had to do was play with a nipple—a suckle or a pinch—and she went off like a rocket.

They probably could have gone for seven, but by then she was exhausted and clenching her legs together, begging him to let her sleep. And he'd figured it was only fair to let her reserve some of her strength for the actual honeymoon.

It was a cool day, so while she took a shower, Sam changed into jeans and a sweater and built a fire in the stone fireplace in the great room. He checked the cupboards and refrigerator and found they were stocked with enough food to last a month.

He was just putting on a kettle for tea when Anne appeared at the top of the stairs, her hair wet and twisted up, held in place with a clip, wearing a black silk robe. Sam couldn't help wondering if she wore anything underneath.

"I know this is a hunting lodge," she said. "But do there have to be so many *dead* things mounted on the walls?"

"Personally, I've never understood the appeal in killing defenseless animals," he told her, watching as she walked down the stairs. When she got the kitchen where he stood, she stopped, looked him up and down and smiled.

"What?" he asked.

"I've never seen you dressed so casually."

"It happens every now and then."

"I like it." She crossed the room to him and rose up to kiss him on the cheek.

She smelled clean and girly and looked delicious enough to eat. He was tempted to scoop her up and carry her off to bed that very instant, or even better, make love to her right there in the kitchen. The butcher-block table looked just the right height for fooling around, although it was pretty rough and scarred from many years of use. He didn't want her getting splinters in her behind. Besides, they had all week. It had been a hectic few days and it would be nice to just relax for a while. Maybe even take a nap. Anne had slept like the dead last night but Sam had tossed and turned, worrying about this Gingerbread Man business.

If something had gone wrong with that bomb, if they had hit a pothole and it had detonated too soon, his uncle and aunt—two of the sweetest people he knew—could have been blown to kingdom come. He agreed with

Anne that something needed to be done, but also saw Chris's point, and he was right, it wasn't worth putting someone's life at risk.

He and Chris would have to have a serious talk when Sam and Anne returned to Thomas Isle. Maybe it was time they considered a new course of action.

"Is everything okay?" Anne asked, her brow wrinkled.

"Of course. Why do you ask?"

"You sort of drifted off there for a second."

He smiled and kissed her forehead. "Just thinking about what a lucky man I am."

She wrapped her arms around his waist and snuggled against him. "I feel lucky, too."

"I was making tea. Would you like a cup?"

"I'd love one. Can I help?"

"You could find some honey. I think I saw it in the cupboard above the coffee maker."

She rooted around in the cupboard while he took two cups and a box of tea bags out.

Suddenly she gasped and stepped back, clutching her belly. "Oh my God!"

Thinking she'd hurt herself, or something was wrong with the baby, he was instantly at her side. "What's the matter? What can I do?"

She looked down at her stomach. "I think I just felt the baby kick."

"You did?"

She nodded excitedly. "When I was pressed up against the cupboard. I've felt flutters before, almost like butterflies in my stomach, but this was different. Like a poke." she said, demonstrating with her index finger on his stomach. "But from the inside. If you press down maybe you can feel it, too."

She unbelted her robe and pulled it open and—*bloody hell*—was naked underneath. She took his hand and pressed his palm firmly over her belly.

"I don't feel anything," he said.

"Shh, just wait a minute." She leaned into him, resting her head against his shoulder.

Looking down, he realized he must have gotten a little carried away last night. She had a few faint love-bites on her breasts. He was willing to bet that he'd find some on her neck as well, and maybe one or two on her inner thighs.

Maybe it was wrong, but with her pressed up against him, smelling so sexy, her skin soft and warm, her breath hot on his neck, he was getting a hard-on. And he definitely wasn't feeling the baby kick. Maybe it was too soon.

He started to move away but she held his hand firmly in place. "Just wait."

He was convinced he *wouldn't* feel anything, and when he actually did—a soft little bump-bump against his palm—he was so startled he almost pulled his hand away.

Her eyes darted up to his. "Did you feel it?"

He laughed in amazement. "I did."

She smiled. "That's our baby, Sam."

He felt it again. Another bump-bump, as if the little guy—or girl—was in there saying, *Hey, here I am.*

He'd heard that for men, feeling their baby move for the first time often made the experience more real, which he'd always thought was total bollocks. It felt

FREE Merchandise is 'in the Cards' for you!

Dear Reader,

We're giving away FREE MERCHANDISE!

Seriously, we'd like to reward you for reading this novel by giving you **FREE MERCHANDISE** worth over **$20**. And no purchase is necessary!

You see the Jack of Hearts sticker above? Paste that sticker in the box on the Free Merchandise Voucher inside. Return the Voucher promptly...and we'll send you valuable Free Merchandise!

Thanks again for reading one of our novels—and enjoy your Free Merchandise with our compliments!

Pam Powers

Pam Powers

P.S. Look inside to see what Free Merchandise is **"in the cards"** for you!

(S-D-08/10)

W

e'd like to send you two free books to introduce you to the Silhouette Desire® series. These books are worth over $10, but they are yours to keep absolutely FREE! We'll even send you 2 wonderful surprise gifts. You can't lose!

REMEMBER: Your Free Merchandise, consisting of **2 Free Books** and **2 Free Gifts**, is worth over $20.00! No purchase is necessary, so please send for your Free Merchandise today.

bloody well real to him the moment she broke the news. But now, after experiencing it, he suddenly realized what they meant. That was *his* baby. No longer just a concept, but something he could feel.

He kept his hand there, hoping it would happen again, but after several minutes more Anne said, "He must be asleep again."

Sam smothered his disappointment and reluctantly pulled his hand away. The kettle had begun to boil, so Anne belted her robe and turned the burner off.

"Why don't we have our tea by the fire?" she suggested.

While he fixed it, she pilfered a fluffy down comforter from one of the beds and spread it out on the floor. He carried their cups over and set them on the hearth.

Anne let her hair down and flopped onto her back, the sides of her robe slipping apart over her belly. Instead of readjusting it, she tugged the belt loose and let the whole thing fall open. He certainly couldn't accuse her of being modest. Even that first night, during the ball, she hadn't been shy about taking it all off. And he could never get tired of looking at her body.

He sat cross-legged facing her, thinking that if the baby started to kick again he would be right there to feel it.

She closed her eyes and sighed contentedly. "The heat from the fire feels nice."

But a little too warm for the sweater he was wearing, so he pulled it up over his head and dropped it on the floor beside him. Anne was looking up at him, smiling.

"What?"

"You have a beautiful body. I like looking at it."

"The feeling is mutual."

"Does it bother you that I'm getting fat?"

He rolled his eyes. "You are *not* getting fat."

"You know what I mean," she said. "My belly is going to get huge."

"And it will look beautiful that way," he assured her, pressing a kiss just above her navel.

"You know, I already found a stretch mark. By the time I give birth I could be covered in them."

He examined her stomach but didn't see anything but smooth, soft skin. "I don't see any stretch marks."

"It's there."

"Where?"

She reached down, feeling around the lowest part of her belly. "Right here...see?"

He leaned in to get a closer look and saw what was, at best, a microscopic imperfection that may or may not have been an actual stretch mark. "It's tiny."

"Yes, but it will probably get bigger, until it's huge."

He seriously doubted that, but her concern surprised him a little. She'd never struck him as the type to be hung up on body image. She seemed so comfortable in her own skin. "You could be covered with them and I wouldn't think you were any less beautiful." He stroked the offending area. Her skin was warm and rosy from the heat coming off the fire. "In fact, I happen to think it's sexy."

She pushed herself up on her elbows. "And I think you're full of bunk."

"I mean it. If I found it off-putting, would I do this?"

He leaned down and kissed the spot, just a soft brush of his lips, and heard her inhale sharply.

When he lifted his head she had that heavy-lidded sleepy look that she got when she was turned on. And seeing her that way gave him an instant erection.

"See," he said.

"I think there might be another one," she said.

"Another stretch mark?"

She nodded solemnly.

"Really?" He manufactured concern. "Where?"

"This one is lower."

"How low?"

"Oh, a couple of inches, maybe."

He knew for a fact that there wasn't one *there,* but he stifled a smile. "I didn't see it."

She put a hand on the back of his head and gently pushed it down. "I think you should look closer."

Enjoying the game, he leaned in and pretended a thorough inspection, close enough that he was sure she could feel the whisper of his breath on her skin. He wasn't sure what the Brazilian wax was doing for her, but he sure was enjoying it.

After a minute or so he shrugged and said. "Sorry, I just don't see it."

He tried to straighten up and she not-so-gently shoved his head back down.

"Look *again.*"

He smiled to himself. "Wait…oh yes, I see it now. Right here." He pressed a kiss right at the apex of her puffy lips, paused, then swept his tongue between them.

Anne moaned and curled her fingers in his hair.

For a brief moment he considered torturing her a bit longer, but the sweet taste of her, her tantalizing scent drew him in like a bee to a flower. Unfortunately his jeans didn't have a lot of give, and he was so hard that a few more minutes of bending over like this was going to do mortal damage. He stretched out beside her in the opposite direction, relieving the pressure, and in a millisecond Anne was tugging at his belt. She worked with impressive speed and in seconds had his erection out of his pants…and into her mouth. It felt so damned fantastic, he might have swallowed his tongue if wasn't already buried in her.

Her mouth was so hot and wet and soft, and the damp ribbons of her hair brushing his stomach and thighs was unbelievably erotic. But when she reached into his jeans and cupped him…well, everything after that was a bit of a blur. A jumble of wet heat and intense pleasure, moans and whimpers that at times he wasn't sure were from him or from her. Or both. Too soon he felt his control slipping, but he never came first. It was against his personal code of conduct. He considered it selfish and impolite. Fortunately, he knew exactly what to do.

When he'd reached the point of no return, he slid a hand up to her breasts, took her nipple between his fingers and squeezed. She moaned, and her body started to quake, which sent him right over the edge with her. He would have cursed in blissful agony if his mouth hadn't been otherwise occupied. Afterward, she collapsed beside him and they lay side by side on the blanket, still facing opposite directions, breathing hard. He felt limp, as though every last bit of energy had been leeched from his body, and the heat from the fire was making him drowsy. Maybe now would be a good time for that nap.

His eyes drifted closed, but he felt Anne sit up beside him.

She gave him a shove. "Hey, wake up."

"I'm tired," he mumbled.

"But I'm not finished with you."

"I can't function. I need rest."

That didn't seem to deter her, because a second later he felt her tugging his jeans down and pulling them off. Now he was exhausted and *naked*. Did she really think that was going to help?

He opened one eye and peered up at her. She flashed him a wicked smile and, starting at his ankles, began kissing and licking her way up his body, and despite his fatigue, he was getting hard again. Apparently she wasn't taking no for an answer this time. And it looked as though that nap would have to wait.

If the perfect honeymoon included staying perpetually naked, eating hastily prepared meals on the floor by the fire and making love on a whim, Sam considered it safe to deem the first three days of their honeymoon a success. In fact, he would be a bit sorry when they had to return to real life.

He lay limp on the blanket in front of the fire, listening to the sound of the shower running overhead. He knew he should probably get up and throw something together for breakfast, as he'd promised Anne he would—the woman had a ravenous appetite lately—but he was so comfortable and relaxed he simply couldn't make himself move. Maybe food could wait, and instead he would pull her back down with him and make love to her one more time first. In the past three days he had mapped and memorized every inch of her, each curve and crevice. There wasn't a place on her body he hadn't caressed and kissed. In fact, it was quite possible that he knew her body better than his own.

What continued to astonish him was that, discounting those four months apart, technically, they had known each other the sum total of less than two weeks. Yet he had never felt so comfortable with a woman. With *anyone,* actually. It was as if they had known one another all their lives. He'd dated his share of women but he had never come close to finding one he could imagine spending the rest of his life with. One who was everything he had ever imagined a wife should be. He was beginning to wonder if he might have found his soul mate. And all because a few intoxicated mates had dared him to ask her to dance.

It was funny how fate worked.

A firm knock on the front door startled him. Sam cursed and pulled himself to his feet, grabbing a throw from the back of the davenport and wrapping it around his waist. As he crossed the room, the words *this better be important* sat on the tip of his tongue, ready to assault whoever was standing on the other side of the door.

The cool air rushing in didn't chill him even close to as much as the look on Gunter's face did. He didn't look upset, exactly. Gunter didn't show emotion. But there was something in his eyes that told Sam this wasn't going to be good news.

"Is urgent call from Prince Christian," Gunter said,

holding out Sam's cell phone. Sam's heart lodged somewhere south of his diaphragm.

"Thank you," he said, taking the phone. Gunter nodded and backed out the door, shutting it behind him. Deep down Sam knew, even before he heard Chris's solemn tone, what the prince was going to say.

"I'm afraid I have some bad news. The king passed away last night."

Sam cursed silently. "Chris, I'm so sorry."

"We'll need you and Anne back at the castle as soon as possible. I'm sure she'll want to see him one last time. Before…"

"Of course."

"Gunter will take you to an airfield not far from the lodge and a chopper will be waiting there. I've already arranged for your things to be brought back separately."

Chris certainly was on top of the situation, and Sam suspected that seeing to all the details was the only thing holding him together.

"Do you want me to tell her, or would you rather do it?" Chris asked.

"I'll tell her."

"Tell me what?" Anne asked.

Sam turned to find Anne standing behind him, wearing her robe, her hair still damp. He hadn't even heard her come down the stairs.

"We'll see you soon," Chris said and disconnected.

"Who was that?" Anne asked as he snapped the phone closed.

"Chris."

"What did he want?" she asked, though her expression said she already suspected.

"I'm afraid he had bad news."

She took a deep breath. "My father?"

He nodded.

"He's gone, isn't he?"

He took her in his arms and held her. "I'm so sorry."

She pressed her cheek against his chest and he could feel that it was already damp. "I'm not ready for this."

"I know." Even if they were ill, and suffering, was anyone ever ready to lose a parent?

Eight

Everyone was surprised to learn that it wasn't a heart attack. The king had just gone to sleep, and sometime in the night his heart had simply stopped beating. According to the physician, he hadn't suffered or felt a thing.

The only solace Anne could take was that he was finally at peace. The last few years had been so hard, and he'd put up one hell of a fight, but he had made peace with the fact that it was his time. Even if his family wasn't ready, he had been.

Chris and Aaron were somber and, like typical men, kept their feelings to themselves. Louisa cried constantly the first day, then miraculously seemed to pull herself together. The worst part was watching her mother cope, knowing that she must have been falling to pieces on the inside, but forcing herself to be strong for her children.

Anne was simply heartbroken. Her father would never know her children, and they would never see firsthand what a wonderful father, and grandfather, what a wonderful *man* he was. It just didn't seem fair that someone with so much to live for should be taken far too soon.

When she checked her e-mail the day of the funeral, reading condolences from friends and relatives, she found one from the Gingerbread Man, too. It said simply, *Boo Hoo.*

Anne had been so furious that she actually picked her laptop up and hurled it at the wall.

Those first few days after the service, she walked around in a fog, functioning on autopilot during the day and falling apart at night in the privacy of their bedroom, crying herself to sleep in Sam's arms while he stroked her hair and murmured soothing words. He was truly a godsend, taking care of her while dealing with the stresses of a new job.

But as the days passed it started to get easier. She began to focus not on her loss, but her new marriage and the baby who seemed to grow exponentially every day. Gradually everyone seemed to get back to their lives. Within a few weeks she and Sam had fallen into a comfortable routine. Before she knew it the day arrived when it was time for her ultrasound.

She drank what felt like *gallons* of water, and by the time they got to the royal family's private wing at the hospital she was in misery. Thank goodness the specialist was in the room and ready for them. When she lay back and exposed her belly he looked a little surprised.

"You're quite large for twenty-one weeks."

"Is that bad?" Sam asked, looking worried.

"Every woman carries differently," the doctor said as he squeezed cold goo on her belly, and used the wand thingy he was holding to spread it around. Images appeared on the screen immediately.

"Hmm." He nodded, his brow furrowed. "That would explain it."

Anne's heart instantly skipped a beat. She simply couldn't handle any more bad news.

"Is something wrong?" Sam asked.

"Not at all. So far everything looks great. I'll have to take a few measurements, but development seems to be just where it should be. For both of them."

At first Anne was confused, thinking he meant her and the baby, then the meaning of his words sank in and she was dumbstruck.

"Are you saying that there are two babies?" Sam asked. "We're having twins?"

The doctor pointed to the screen. "This is baby A, and over here is baby B."

"But there was only one heartbeat," Anne said.

"It's not uncommon for the hearts to beat in unison, making it difficult to differentiate between them. I'm sure your doctor explained that because you're a twin it was more likely you would have twins."

"Of course, but…"

"I guess that explains why you're so big already," Sam said, sounding surprisingly calm about this. In fact, while she was stunned, he looked as though he couldn't be happier.

"Would you like to know the sex of the babies?"

the doctor asked. She and Sam said "yes" in unison, then laughed because they were obviously very much in agreement.

"We'll see if we can get them to cooperate," he said, trying different angles. Then he pointed to the screen. "See there. This is baby A. There's the left leg, and the right, and see that protrusion in between?"

"A boy!" Sam said, beaming.

Baby B didn't want to cooperate, so he had Anne turn on her side, so the babies would shift position. "There we go!" the doctor finally said, pointing out both legs again, and there was no little protrusion this time.

"A girl," Anne said excitedly, squeezing Sam's hand. "One of each!"

The doctor took the measurements he needed and announced that everything looked wonderful. Her children were healthy, Sam was beaming with pride, and Anne could say with certainty that it was one of the happiest days of her life. After all that had happened lately, she figured they deserved it.

When the doctor was finished Anne dashed to the loo to empty her bladder before it burst. When she met Sam in the waiting room, he had an odd look on his face.

What if the idea of having twins had finally sunk in and he'd realized it was more than he bargained for? What if he was overwhelmed by the responsibility?

"What's wrong, Sam?"

"The doctor and I had an interesting discussion while you were gone."

"What kind of discussion? Is something wrong with the babies?"

"I voiced some concerns about you being on birth

control when you conceived. I was afraid it might cause complications or defects."

Anne's breath hitched. "What did he say?"

"He checked your chart."

Oh God. Anne's heart sank so hard and fast it left a hollow feeling in her chest. "Sam—"

"I want the truth, Anne. That night, when you said you had it covered, did you mean it, or did you lie to me?"

It felt as though the entire room had flipped on its axis and she had to grab the wall to keep from pitching over. "I can explain—"

"Did. You. *Lie*." He was angry. Not just angry, but seething mad. This man who had never so much as raised his voice looked as though he wanted to throttle her.

She had to force the words past the lump of fear blocking her throat. "Yes, but—"

The door opened and Gunter stuck his head in to tell them the car was ready.

"Sam," she said, but he silenced her with a sharp look and said, "When we get home."

The ride back to the castle was excruciating. Sam sat silently beside her, but she could feel his anger. It seemed to fill the car, until it became difficult to breathe. Or maybe that was her guilty conscience.

There had to be a way to fix this. To make him understand.

When they got back they went straight to their room and Sam closed the door firmly behind him. Then he turned to her and in a voice teeming with bitterness said, "I should have known."

"Sam…" She tried to touch his arm but he jerked it away.

"I was raised on the principle that royals are never to be trusted, that they always have an agenda. I knew it that night, and still I ignored my instincts."

It crushed her that he would ever think of her that way. Yet she couldn't deny she slept with him knowing they were unprotected. "It's not what you think. I didn't have any agenda. I wasn't trying to trap you."

"So, you just wanted sex."

He made it sound so sleazy. He had been there, too, he knew damn well how deeply they had connected. He had wanted her, too. "I wanted you, Sam, and I honestly didn't think I would get pregnant. The timing was completely off."

"So what you're saying is, with no regard to anyone but yourself and your own selfish needs, you took a chance. You didn't even have the decency to stop and consider the repercussions of your actions, and how it might affect me."

When he said it that way, it *was* pretty awful.

"I'm sorry," she said in a whisper, because suddenly she couldn't seem to draw in a full breath, as though his animosity was leeching all the oxygen from the air.

"You're *sorry*," he said, spitting out a rueful laugh. "You stole *everything* from me and all you can say is you're sorry?"

"I made a mistake. I know. But I love you, Sam."

"You love me?" he said, astonished. "Playing Russian roulette with my future? Lying to me? You call that *love?* I think there's only one person here that you give a damn about, Your Highness, and that's you."

He couldn't be more wrong. She hated herself right now. For not having the guts to tell him the truth right away. "Sam, I just wanted—"

"You wanted to screw me," he said. "And I guess you succeeded because as far as I can see, I am thoroughly screwed."

He yanked the door open and stormed out, slamming it behind him.

Anne's heart was pounding and she was trembling so hard her legs wouldn't hold her upright. She slid down the wall to the floor, her legs finally folding under her like a marionette whose strings had been cut.

Sam was right. Everything he said about her was true, and he had every right to be furious with her. But was he mad enough to leave her? To demand a divorce?

Maybe after he had some time to cool down and think things through, he would remember how happy he'd been and how good they were together.

And what if he didn't? What then?

The worst part was that she had no one to blame for this mess but herself. And the happiest day in her life had just turned into her worst nightmare.

Anne didn't know where Sam went, but she learned from Gunter that he took his own car and left without a bodyguard. Which, considering the Gingerbread Man's escalating violence, probably wasn't the smartest idea, but she was in no position to be telling him what to do.

He had arranged to take the afternoon off for the ultrasound, so she knew he probably wasn't at the office. He could be anywhere. And even if she did know where he went, there was nothing she could do about it. She needed to give him space, time to think things through.

She wasn't the least bit hungry, but with two babies growing inside her, she knew skipping meals wasn't an option. But since she didn't feel like facing her family—and any questions—she asked Geoffrey to bring her dinner to her room. She was so beside herself she couldn't choke more than a few bites down.

To kill time while she waited for Sam, she started a list of all the baby things they were going to have to get. They would need two of everything. And they were going to have to think about names. It still amazed her that she was having twins, and she realized her family didn't even know yet. But that was the kind of news she and Sam should announce together.

A little later Louisa knocked on her door and Anne called for her to come in.

"I'm not disturbing you, am I?" Louisa asked, peeking her head in and looking around for Sam.

"I'm alone."

She stepped inside. "Oh, where's Sam?"

If she told Louisa they'd had a fight, she would have to tell her why, and she was too ashamed to admit how badly she had screwed things up.

"He had a thing with his parents," she said, keeping it vague. "I was supposed to go, but I wasn't feeling well."

Louisa frowned. "Are you all right?"

"Fine, just normal pregnancy stuff."

She flopped down on the bed beside her. "Is that why you didn't come down for dinner?"

"I had Geoffrey bring me a tray."

"Mother ate with us again."

"That's good," Anne said. For months now, since their father became so ill, he and their mother shared dinner in their suite. And right after the funeral she continued to eat alone, until they all finally talked her into coming back down to the dining room.

"She told Chris that she thinks he and Melissa and the triplets should move into the master suite. Since he is king now. And there's five of them and just one of her."

"What did he say?"

"At first he said no, but she insisted, so he said he would think about it. Maybe she just has too many memories there."

"She shouldn't rush into anything. It hasn't even been a month. She needs to give herself time to grieve."

"I agree, but try telling her that. And people wonder where we got our stubborn streak."

One of the babies rolled and Anne placed a hand on her belly.

"Kicking?" Louisa asked, putting a hand beside Anne's. She loved feeling the baby move.

"More like rolling."

"I wish I were pregnant, too," she said, looking sad.

"It'll happen. It's only been a few months. Sometimes it takes a while." And sometimes it worked on the first shot, whether she wanted it to or not.

"Well, it's certainly not for a lack of trying. Last night alone—"

"Please," Anne interrupted. "Spare me the gory details. I believe you."

Louisa grinned. "I'm pushing thirty. If I'm going to have six kids, I have to get the ball rolling. Besides, don't you think it would be fun if we were pregnant together?"

"We still could be. I've got nineteen weeks to go." Although maybe less, because the doctor said it wasn't uncommon for twins to come as much as four weeks early. That meant she and Sam could be parents in only *fifteen* weeks.

"Well, if not this time then the next," Louisa said with a shrug. But Anne didn't tell her there wouldn't be a next time. She hadn't even been sure she wanted *one* child. Two kids, especially since she was having one of each gender, was going to be her limit.

She wanted so badly to tell Louisa about the ultrasound. It was right there on the tip of her tongue, dying to come out, but she restrained herself. She and Sam should tell everyone together and she didn't think it was fair to deprive him of that. And she didn't want to give him yet another reason to be mad at her.

After Louisa left—probably to work on making that baby with Garrett—Anne picked up a novel she'd been meaning to start. Even though it was written by one of her favorite authors, she just couldn't concentrate. Her mind kept wandering and her eyes drifting to the clock on the bedside table.

It was going on eleven. Where could he be?

At midnight she finally changed into her pajamas and crawled into bed, but she couldn't sleep. It was after one when Sam finally opened the bedroom door and stepped inside.

Her heart stalled, then picked up double-time.

He went to the closet to change, the light cutting a path though the darkness. Then the light went out and she heard him in the bathroom. The shower turned on and she lay in the darkness listening and waiting. Finally the bathroom door opened, the light went out and he walked to the bed. She could smell the scent of soap and shampoo as he climbed in beside her.

For a long moment she lay silent, afraid to make a sound, afraid that he was still angry. She waited to see if he made the first move, but after several minutes he hadn't said a word. Maybe he thought she was asleep.

She rolled on her side facing him and asked, "Can we talk about this?"

"There's nothing to talk about."

"Sam…" She laid a hand on his arm but he shrugged it away. "Please."

"Nothing you could say or do will erase what you did to me."

His words cut deep and she realized he wasn't even close to being ready to forgive her. "I understand. So long as you know that when you're ready to talk, I'll be here."

He sat up suddenly and switched on the light, blinding her for a second. When her eyes adjusted she saw that he looked tired, and angry and…betrayed. "You don't get it. I know what you did, and why you did it, and nothing you can say will ever change it. You stole my life from me. It's done. I'm not just going to get over it."

Her heart sank. He didn't even want to try to forgive

her? To understand her side of it? He was just going to give up?

She had grown to love Sam, but obviously for him, she was as easily discarded as a used tissue. "So what are you saying? That it's over?"

"We both know that isn't an option. Like you said, once we're married, that's it. Royals don't do divorce."

Her relief was all encompassing. And it must have shown because he added hastily, "Don't think for a second that I'm doing this for you. I'm staying married to you for my children. That's it."

Yes, but as long as he was still there, still a part of her life, he would eventually have to forgive her. He couldn't stay mad forever.

"I didn't tell anyone our news yet," she said. "About the twins. I thought we should announce it together."

"You needn't have bothered waiting. I already told my parents. Tell your family whenever and whatever you want. It really doesn't matter to me."

His words cut so deep, she wouldn't have been surprised to find blood on her pajamas.

With that he switched off the light and lay back down, turning his back to her. A clear indication that the conversation was now over. Though her stubborn, argumentative side wanted to push, she forced herself to let it go. She just needed to give him time. Eventually he would remember how happy they'd been, how good they were together.

Sam may have never said he loved her, but she knew he did. She could feel it. And people didn't fall out of love instantly. The fact that he was feeling so angry and betrayed was a sure sign that he cared deeply for her. Otherwise it wouldn't matter what she had done to him.

It simply had to work out. Because the alternative was not an option.

Nine

How had Sam gotten himself into this mess?

He sat at his desk, in his new office—which he couldn't deny was far larger and more lavish than even his father's, with a secretary on the other side of the door who had already proven herself more than competent—contemplating the disaster that was now his life.

Their marriage was supposed to be perfect. And it had been. They had been happy. Right up until the instant he learned that it was all a lie.

People had always accused him of being too laid-back and easygoing. Too trusting, especially for a politician. But he had always considered it one of his strengths. Now it would seem that everyone had been right, and his ignorance had finally come back to bite him in the ass.

However, that wasn't a mistake he intended to make again.

All he'd ever wanted was a marriage like his parents had. He wanted a partner and a soul mate. He wasn't naive enough to believe there wouldn't be occasional disagreements or spats. That he could live with. But what Anne had done to him was unforgivable. And not just the part when she lied about the birth control. She'd had a chance to redeem herself and tell him the truth when she came to tell him about the baby. Instead she had lied to him again. And she kept lying.

Now he was trapped in a marriage with a wife he could never trust. Never love, even if he'd wanted to. And he had been close. So close that the thought of his gullibility sickened him.

At least something good had come out of this miserable union. Three things actually. His son and his daughter. He would never consider a child anything but a blessing—no matter the circumstances of its conception—and he would never hold them responsible for their mother's deception.

The third good thing was his job with the royal family. He'd always been a people person, and in his new position as foreign ambassador, communication was the main thrust of his position. He actually looked forward to going to work every morning. Even before it meant getting away from his wife. So of course the last thing he wanted to do was put that position in jeopardy. And despite what Anne had done to him, he didn't doubt her family would take her side. Sam could easily find himself working out of an office the size of a closet pushing papers. Or even worse, they might delegate him to work in their agricultural department, possibly picking weeds in the fields, so he figured it was in his best interest not to let anyone know that he and Anne were, for all intents and purposes, estranged.

But it wasn't easy to play the doting newlywed husband when he was so filled with resentment. And though he hadn't yet discussed it with Anne, he was quite sure she would agree to the charade. She owed him that at least.

It had taken him hours to finally fall asleep last night, and when he woke this morning he almost reached for her, the way he usually did. Making love in the mornings had become a part of their regular routine.

Then he remembered what she had done and rolled out of bed instead.

He didn't doubt that he would miss the sex. When it came to sexual compatibility, they were off the charts. But he couldn't abide by having sex with a woman whom he no longer respected. One he didn't even like.

She had still been sleeping, or pretending to, when he left for work. He usually ate breakfast with the family, but he'd had no appetite this morning. Now it was barely eight-thirty and he'd already been in the office forty-five minutes. But it was better than being at home. With her.

At nine Chris knocked on his door. "I hear congratulations are in order."

Sam must have looked confused, because Chris added, "Twins?"

"Oh, right!" Of course, Anne must have told them this morning.

Chris laughed. "Don't tell me you forgot."

"No, I just…" He shook his head. "Busy morning. And I didn't sleep well last night."

"As the parent of triplets, I can tell you it's not quite as daunting as it sounds. Not yet anyway. Get back to me when they're teenagers."

"It was definitely a surprise, but we're both thrilled." At least, she had seemed thrilled. Until the walls caved in on them.

"And like Anne said, you get one of each, so you don't have to go through this again."

A wise decision in light of the situation. Not that he'd have wanted more than that anyway. Two was a nice tidy number. It seemed to suit his parents fairly well. Although he was sure his mother would have liked a little girl to spoil. He was sure a granddaughter would be the next best thing. And he was happy to be able to give her that.

"Of course," Chris added, "I understand some women enjoy being pregnant. Melissa was carrying three, so it wasn't the easiest of pregnancies. But Anne seems to be doing well."

Sam wasn't sure how Anne felt about being pregnant. Other than a few halfhearted gripes about stretch marks and occasional complaints about heartburn, if she had reservations, he didn't hear about them. Even when she was getting sick she didn't grumble about it. Truth be told, she was fairly low maintenance for a princess. "I imagine it will get uncomfortable closer to her due date. Her only concern at this point seems to be stretch marks."

"That was a big issue for Melissa, too. But it's kind

of an inevitability with multiples, I think. Mel has a list of plastic surgeons she's considering already."

"I guess that means you're stopping at three?"

"Neither of us wants to take another spin on the fertility roller coaster."

It struck Sam as ironic that Chris and Melissa had worked so hard to have a child, while Sam and Anne, who weren't even trying, hit the jackpot the first time. Maybe she had been thinking the same thing that night. Not that it was an excuse to put his future on the line without his knowledge. If she had been honest and said that she wasn't taking birth control, but the timing was off and she most likely wasn't fertile, he might have said what the hell and slept with her anyway. But that would have been *his* choice. She had deprived him of that.

Chris's cell phone rang, and when he looked at the display said, "It's Garrett."

He answered, and not ten seconds into the conversation Sam could see by his expression that something was wrong.

He listened, nodding solemnly, then asked, "Were there any injuries?"

Sam sat a little straighter is his chair. Had there been another incident?

"How bad?" Chris asked. He listened for another minute, his expression increasingly grim, then said, "I'll be right over."

He shut his phone and told Sam, "I have to get to the east field greenhouse facility."

Sam knew that was the heart of the royal family's vast organic farming business. When an unidentifiable blight infected the crops there last year, it put the economic fate of the entire island in jeopardy.

"Did something happen there?" he asked.

"Yeah, it just blew up."

It was a bomb identical to the one detonated at Anne and Sam's wedding, activated remotely from God only knew where, and was hidden in the men's loo. The force actually shot a commode through the roof and it had come crashing down on a car parked in the lot several hundred feet away. Thankfully an *empty* car. But half a dozen people were injured in the blast, two of them with third-degree burns, and one with shrapnel to his eye that could possibly cost him his sight. The greenhouse itself had sustained hundreds of thousands of pounds' worth of damage.

A busload of school children had been scheduled to tour the facility only an hour later and Anne shuddered to think what would have happened if he'd detonated the bomb then. That alone was cause for great relief as the family gathered in the study after dinner the following night to discuss the investigation. The only other bright spot in this tragic situation was that this time the Gingerbread Man had made a crucial error. He'd allowed himself to be caught on surveillance. And not just the top of his head this time. This was a straight-on, up-close-and-personal view of his face.

He'd entered the facility the previous day posing as a repairman. He had the proper credentials so no one seemed to think twice about letting him in. He wore a cap, and kept his head down so that the brim covered his face. It was sheer dumb luck that, on his way out, someone carrying a large piece of equipment bumped into him in the hallway, hitting his cap and knocking it off his head. For a split second he jerked his head up and just happened to be standing under a surveillance camera. If they had planned it, it couldn't have been more eloquent.

"He's not the monster I expected," Louisa said, looking at the still shot of his face that had been taken from the tape. It had already been distributed to the authorities and would run on the national news. Someone would recognize him, meaning it was only a matter of time before he was identified and apprehended.

"He looks…intense," Liv said, taking the photo from Louisa to study it. "It's his eyes, I think. There's an intelligence there."

"If he's so intelligent," Aaron quipped, "why did he make a mistake?"

"Intelligent or not, it was inevitable that he would eventually screw up," Chris said, taking the photo, giving it another quick look, then setting it on the bar before he walked over to sit next to their mother on the settee. "This nightmare is almost over."

"This would have pleased your father," she said with a sad smile. "It's about time we had some good news. We should have a toast, to celebrate. Don't you think?"

"I'm all for a little celebrating," Aaron said.

"I'm sure we could scrounge up a bottle or two of champagne," Chris said, ringing Geoffrey.

"Champagne please, Geoffrey," their mother said, when he stepped into the room.

Geoffrey nodded and said, "Of course, Your Highness."

"Water for me," Anne told him.

"Me, too," Melissa added as he walked to the bar.

"I thought you stopped nursing," Louisa said.

"I did. But champagne makes me groggy and I have to be up for a 2:00 a.m. feeding."

That would be her and Sam in a few months, Anne thought, and she could only hope their situation had improved by then. And as much as she wanted the Gingerbread Man caught, it was difficult to feel like celebrating.

All evening Sam had acted as if nothing was out of the ordinary, but she knew that was for her family's sake. They had agreed that it would be best if they kept up the ruse of being happily married newlyweds. The kind who no longer had sex. Or *spoke*. At least she would be spared the humiliation of having to admit that barely a month after their wedding they were already having issues.

There was a sudden crash behind the bar and everyone turned simultaneously to look.

"My apologies," Geoffrey said, leaning down to clean up the glass he'd dropped. Anne was standing close by so she walked around to help him, picking up some of the larger pieces. She noticed, as he swept the smaller shards into a dustpan, that his hands were shaking, and when he stood, his face looked pale.

She took his hand. It was ice cold. "Are you okay?"

"Arthritis," he said apologetically, gently extracting it from her grasp.

She helped him pour the champagne and when everyone had a glass they toasted to the new lead in the investigation.

"I have an excellent idea," their mother said. "You kids should play poker. It is Friday."

Everyone exchanged a look. Friday used to be poker night, but since the king's death they hadn't played.

"We could do that," Chris said.

"I'm in," Aaron piped in, then he turned to Sam. "Do you play?"

"Not since college, but I'm pretty sure I remember how."

Like sharks smelling fresh blood in the water, Chris and Aaron grinned.

"Count me in, too," Garrett said.

"I think I'll head down to the lab instead," Liv said.

"You don't play poker?" Sam asked her.

"We don't let her," Aaron said, shooting her a grin. "She cheats."

Liv gave him a playful shove, her cheeks turning a bright shade of pink. "I do not!"

"She counts cards," Aaron said.

"Not on purpose," she told Sam. "It's just that when it comes to numbers I have a photographic memory."

"How about you, Anne?" Chris asked. "You up for a game?"

Though Anne normally played, she figured it might be a better idea to give Sam some space. Maybe relaxing with her brothers, not to mention a few drinks, would make him forget how angry he was with her. "I don't think so."

"Why don't you help me get the triplets ready for bed," Melissa suggested. "For practice. After that, having two babies will feel easy."

"I'd love to."

"I'll help, too!" Louisa said excitedly.

"I thought we could watch a movie," their mother said.

"Of course," Louisa said with a bright smile, though Anne guessed that deep down she preferred to help Melissa.

Everyone went their separate ways and Anne followed Melissa to the nursery.

"Have you decided if you're taking the master suite?" Anne asked her.

"I don't know. It just seems like it should belong to the queen."

"Have you forgotten that you *are* the queen?" When Chris became king, Melissa automatically became queen, and their mother was given the title of Queen Mother. Which was technically more of a lateral move than a demotion.

"It's just really hard to fathom," Melissa said. "Three years ago I didn't even know I was a royal. But I can't deny it would be nice to have all the space."

Instead of going into the nursery, Melissa walked past it to her and Chris's bedroom and opened the door.

Anne stopped, confused. "I thought…"

"The nanny put them to bed already. I wanted to talk to you, and I didn't want to say anything in front of everyone else." She gestured Anne inside.

Anne got a sinking feeling in her chest. Was she so transparent that Melissa had figured out something was wrong? Or had she heard Anne and Sam fighting the other night?

They sat on the sofa by the window and Anne held

her breath. If Melissa did ask about Sam, what would Anne say? She didn't want to lie, but she had promised Sam, for the sake of his job, not to tell anyone.

"I wanted to talk to you about something. About Louisa."

Anne felt a mix of relief and confusion. "Louisa? What did she do?"

"Oh, she didn't do anything. It's just…something happened." She stopped and sighed.

"What happened?"

"Chris and I are going to be making an announcement, and I'm afraid she's going to be upset. I talked to your mother, but she suggested I talk to you. You know Louisa better than anyone. I thought maybe you could think of a way that we could…soften the blow."

"What could you possibly have to say that would make her so up—" She gasped when she realized there really was only one thing. "Oh my God! Melissa, are you *pregnant?*"

She bit her lip and nodded. "I took a test today."

"Already?" She laughed. The triplets were barely four months old.

"This obviously wasn't planned. I was all ready to schedule my tummy tuck. After the fertility hell we went through, and the in vitro, I didn't think I could even get pregnant naturally. Not to mention that you're not supposed to be able to get pregnant while you're nursing. As far as I can tell, it had the opposite effect on me. If we had known it was even a possibility we would have been a lot more careful."

"How far along are you?"

"Probably four or five weeks."

"So your children will be almost exactly a year apart."

"Don't remind me," she groaned.

"Six babies born within a year." Anne shook her head in disbelief. "We're going to have to build another wing onto the castle."

"Which is why I'm worried about Louisa. She's so desperate to get pregnant. Have you looked at Garrett lately? The poor guy is exhausted."

"Yeah, but he's always smiling."

"Still, she's so…fragile. I'm afraid this might put her over the edge."

That was a common misconception. But Louisa was a lot tougher that she let people think. "First off, Louisa is not that fragile. And second, if the tables were turned, you know she wouldn't hesitate to announce her news to the entire world. Even if that meant hurting someone's feelings."

Melissa nodded. "You've got a point."

"Louisa has never been a patient person. When she wants something, she doesn't like to wait for it. But she and Garrett have only been trying for a couple of months. It can take time. She's going to have to accept that."

"So you really think I shouldn't worry?"

"I do. And if she does get upset, she'll get over it."

"Thank you," she said, taking Anne's hand and giving it a squeeze.

They talked about Anne's pregnancy for a while, and she pretended that everything was okay. That she wasn't miserable and scared. It had only been two days, but what if Sam really couldn't forgive her? Could she stay with a man who resented her so? Would she even want to?

When he came to bed that night she was already under the covers but wide-awake. He didn't say a word. He just crawled in beside her, facing away. She wasn't sure how relaxing the game had been, but she could tell from the whiff of alcohol that he'd been drinking. Still, he didn't even kiss her good-night. On top of that, she had a case of heartburn that wouldn't quit and her back was aching. She slept in fits and starts, and finally crawled out of bed around six-thirty and wandered down to the kitchen for a glass of milk.

She was surprised to find Chris there, still in his pajamas, drinking coffee and reading the paper.

"You're up early," she said, pouring herself a glass of milk.

"It was my morning for the 4:00 a.m. feeding," he said, setting the paper aside. "Then I couldn't get back to sleep. I'll be very happy when the triplets are sleeping through the night."

"Isn't that what you have nannies for?"

"Only to assist. Mel and I agreed that if we were going to have children, we wouldn't rely on the hired help to do all the dirty work."

"Excuse me, Your Highness."

They both turned to see Geoffrey standing in the doorway to his residence behind the kitchen. He looked terrible. His hair was mussed, his eyes red and puffy, as though he hadn't slept a wink all night. Though she had never once seen him emerge in anything but his uniform, he was wearing a velour robe over flannel pajamas. The idea that maybe he really was sick made her heart sink. Chris looked concerned, as well.

"I was hoping to have a word with you," Geoffrey said.

"Of course, Geoffrey, what is it?"

He walked over to where they stood. He had a sheet of paper clutched in his hand. The surveillance photo of the Gingerbread Man, she realized. He set it down on the countertop.

"I need to speak with security, about this photo."

"You recognize him?" Anne asked.

Geoffery nodded. "I do."

"Who is he?" Chris asked.

"This man," he said, in an unsteady voice, "is my son."

Ten

His name was Richard Corrigan.

The entire family was shocked and saddened at learning he was Geoffrey's son, but at least now they had a good idea what had started this whole thing.

According to Richard's mother, whom Geoffrey contacted immediately, he had always deeply resented the royal family. Especially the children, whom he felt his father had chosen over him. But his bitterness didn't manifest into violence until recently.

He was Special Forces in the military and highly decorated, until an assignment gone terribly wrong in Afghanistan, where he saw many of his fellow soldiers brutally slain, left him suffering from PTSD. Rather than giving him the counseling he needed, he was discharged from the service instead. Apparently he snapped, and started to blame the royal family for his troubles.

The reference to the nursery rhymes, Geoffrey suspected, dated back to when Richard was small and he would read to him. He admitted that deep down he suspected it might be his son months ago, but he hadn't wanted to believe it. He thought it might be his own guilty conscience playing tricks on him. Only when he saw the photo could he no longer deny the truth.

In his guilt and grief Geoffrey tried to quit, but no one would accept his resignation. He was a part of the family and families stuck together. Chris assured him that when Richard was apprehended, he would see to it personally that he got the psychiatric help he needed.

Unfortunately, after a month, and a worldwide bulletin calling for his capture, he hadn't been arrested. There had been dozens of reported sightings and tips called in, but none of them panned out.

Anne couldn't help thinking that their champagne celebration had been hasty and they may have jinxed themselves irrevocably. And though she wanted to believe that he would be caught before he detonated another bomb and hurt more people, her life in general was in such a shamble, she couldn't help but expect the worst.

It had been a long and miserable month since their fight, but Sam still hadn't come around. It wasn't even that he was bitter or unkind. At least to that she had defenses. What she couldn't bear, what was slowly eating away at her, was the indifference. The silence. They only spoke when it was necessary, and even then she usually got one-word answers from him. He often worked late, or went out for drinks with his friends. He kept up the ruse of their happy marriage in front of her family, for which she was infinitely grateful, but otherwise, he ignored her.

She didn't understand how he could go from being so sweet and attentive to acting as though she didn't exist. Was it really so easy for him to shut her out, to flip his emotions on and off like a light switch?

In a month he hadn't so much as kissed her, and though she had tried a few time to initiate sex, she was met with icy indifference. She suspected that given the choice, he would opt to not share a bed with her any longer. What was the point when he had drawn a very distinct and bold invisible line down the center of their mattress? But it was her experience that men could only go so long without sex before they explored alternative options, and she couldn't help worrying that it was only a matter of time before he came home smelling of another woman's perfume.

For that reason alone, and despite the indignity of his perpetual cold shoulder, she continued to try to seduce him. She waited until nights when she knew he was in a particularly good mood, when his defenses might be down. She kept thinking that if they made love, reminded him how good it used to be, it would make him want to forgive her.

She kept telling herself that if she was persistent, eventually he would give in, and if she kept him sexually satisfied, he wouldn't think about straying. Even if he couldn't love her, at least he would be faithful.

Then she began to wonder if he was refusing her advances not because of their fight, but because he was completely turned off by her body. Maybe, with her huge belly and expanding hips, she disgusted him to the point that he couldn't stand to even touch her. Maybe their fight had been a convenient excuse to act on feelings he'd been having as far back as their honeymoon.

With the seed planted, the idea began to fester, until she became convinced Sam was disgusted by her body. Until the sight of her own reflection in the mirror disturbed and humiliated her. She stopped undressing in front of him and began showering with the lights off so she wouldn't have to look at herself.

She had never been one of those women with body issues. She had always been comfortable in her own skin, and didn't particularly care what anyone thought. Being in the public eye, Anne found that people didn't hesitate to voice their very critical opinions. Now it consumed her thoughts. She dressed in baggy clothes and oversize sweaters to hide the grotesque curves.

She had herself so convinced that she was hideous that she gave up on trying to seduce Sam. She threw in the towel and resigned herself to the inevitable. Eventually he was going to find someone else to satisfy him sexually. They were going to be one of *those* couples. The kind who kept up the ruse of their marriage for appearances, even when rumors of infidelity became common knowledge. In public people would stare and whisper behind her back. Sam's friends would be polite to her face and snicker when she was out of earshot.

"Poor Princess Anne," they would say. "Too naive to realize she's been played the fool."

The possibility was like the final hit to the spike that he had slowly been driving through her heart.

Anne had been going to bed earlier and earlier lately, so when Sam came home late from work one evening, he wasn't surprised to hear that at nine, she had already gone upstairs.

After a quick bite in the kitchen, and a short conversation with Chris about the conference call they had both stayed late for, Sam headed upstairs. He expected Anne to be asleep already, but the bed was empty. He walked into the closet to change out of his suit and heard the shower running. The bathroom door was open a crack, and he had to fight the urge to peek inside, to get a glimpse of her.

Despite everything that had happened, he was still sexually attracted to Anne, still desired her with an intensity that sometimes had him taking cold showers to control his urges and waking in the middle of the night in a cold sweat.

Lying beside her every night, not touching her, was a special kind of torture. It had taken more strength than he thought he possessed to keep turning down her overtures. But he didn't feel it was fair to make love to her, to give her hope that things might change, when he knew that wasn't true.

He knew he was making her miserable, and despite what she probably believed, that wasn't his intention. Since they were stuck with each other, he had hoped they would reach an understanding, find some middle ground where they could coexist peacefully. But his life was anything but peaceful.

It had been almost two weeks since she'd initiated sex; she'd even gone so far as to stop undressing in front of him, which he'd thought would be a relief. Instead, the longer he went without seeing her, or touching her, he wanted her that much more. But giving in, making love to her, would just do more damage.

He walked closer to the bathroom door, thinking he would just accidentally bump it with his elbow while he hung up his suit jacket. But when he did, he still couldn't see a thing. The room was black as pitch.

What would possess her to shower with all the lights off?

Puzzled, he walked into the bedroom to drop his watch and phone on the bedside table. Then he remembered that he had to be to work early for another conference call and set the alarm on his phone for six-thirty. He walked back into the closet, tugging his shirt off, and saw that Anne was out of the shower and drying off with her back to him. Seeing her naked again made him hard instantly. She dropped the towel and turned his way, shrieking when she saw him standing there.

At first he thought he'd only startled her, until she reached down and clawed at the ground for the towel she'd just dropped. She fumbled to untwist it, holding it up to cover herself, a look of sheer horror on her face.

She acted as if he were a rapist or molester. The fact that he had seen her frequently, and intimately, naked made her reaction more than a little peculiar. He was so surprised his first instinct was to ask, "What the hell is the matter with you?"

His harsh tone made her flinch. "I…I'm sorry. I didn't know you were here."

What did she think she was doing? Punishing him by not letting him see her undressed? Torturing him? Well, he had news for her. It was torture no matter what she did. Dressed, undressed, he still wanted her.

She fumbled with the towel, trying to cover as much of herself as possible, and something inside him snapped. What right did she have to deprive him of anything? Damn it, she *owed* him.

He reached out, fisted the towel and yanked it away from her. She tried desperately to shield his view with her hands, looking around for something to cover herself, deep red splotches blooming across her cheeks.

She was embarrassed, he realized. Not just embarrassed, but mortified. "Anne, what is the matter with you?"

"I'm fat," she said in a wobbly voice, tears gathering in the corners of her eyes. "My body is disgusting."

Suddenly it all made sense. The reason she didn't undress in front of him. And why she showered with the lights off. She was ashamed of her body. A woman who, six weeks ago, had no issue walking around naked, flaunting herself to him.

If she were anyone else, he might have suspected it was an act, to make him feel guilty for ignoring her. But she'd had weeks to pull that sort of stunt. This was real.

He had finally done it. He had broken her. He'd taken a woman who was sharp and feisty and full of life and he had shattered her spirit. He'd made her hate herself and he hated *himself* for it.

And he could no longer live with himself if he didn't fix it.

When Sam came toward her he looked so furious that, for a terrifying second, she thought he was going to hit her. She even put her hands up to shield herself. But instead he swooped her up in his arms, which, despite her added tonnage, he did effortlessly. Only then, with her hip pressed against his pelvis, did she realize that he was erect.

Was that what it took to arouse him? Exposing and humiliating her?

He carried her into the bedroom and dropped her on the bed, right on top of the covers. She tried to pull the duvet up over herself and he yanked it back into place. Then he started unfastening his pants.

"Wh-what are you doing?" she asked, and cursed herself for sounding so fragile and weak. So afraid. She was tougher than this.

"What does it look like I'm doing?"

"I—I don't want to."

"You've obviously got some warped version of reality and I feel obligated to set you straight." He shoved his pants down and kicked them away. "Not touching you has been the *worst* kind of torture. But I restrained myself. I thought it wasn't fair to lead you on, to make you think that anything was going to change. But I can see now that I've only made things worse."

She was afraid to say a word. To even open her mouth. He got on the bed and lowered himself over her, his familiar weight pressing her into the mattress. It felt so good, she could have cried.

"This changes nothing," he said firmly. "Not about our relationship, or the way I feel about you. You understand that?"

She understood it, even if she couldn't accept it. But she missed him so badly, she didn't care what happened after tonight. She just wanted to touch him, to feel him inside her. There was a huge lump in her throat, and she feared that if she tried to talk she would start to cry, so she nodded instead.

"You are a beautiful woman, Anne. I'm sorry if my actions made you think otherwise." He lowered his head and kissed her. Hard. He centered himself between her legs and drove into her, deep and rough, again and again, almost as if he were trying to punish her. But it was so wonderful, such a relief to know he still wanted her, tears leaked from the corners of her eyes. Almost instantly her body began to shudder with release and Sam wasn't far behind her. She didn't want it to be over so fast, she wanted to be close to him, then she realized, he wasn't finished. She barely had a chance to catch her breath before he began thrusting into her again, still hard. He lasted longer this time, making her come twice before he let himself climax. And after what couldn't have been more than a moment or two of rest, he was ready to go again. It was almost as if his body was making up for lost time and refused to rest until it had its fill of her, and her own body accepted him eagerly.

They eventually fell asleep in a sweaty tangle. Then sometime in the middle of the night she woke to feel his hand between her legs, stroking her. She moaned and pulled him to her, and they made love again.

Eleven

When Anne woke the next morning Sam was already up, and she could hear the shower running. She lay there waiting for him. She had never been so physically satisfied, and was feeling a troubling combination of joy and dread.

Never had sex been as passionate as last night. But what now? Would he go back to ignoring her? Would they only connect at night between the sheets of their bed? And could she live with that? Was it even worth it?

She heard the shower stop, then the bathroom door opened. She heard him moving around in the closet. He came out a few minutes later, a towel riding low on his hips, his hair damp and curly. She held her breath, waiting to see what he would do. If he would talk to her, or move through his morning routine without a word, the way he had been for weeks.

He walked over to his side of the bed, sat on the edge of the mattress. He sat there for thirty seconds or so, not saying a word, then finally turned to face her. "I'm tired of holding on to my anger. It's exhausting and it's not doing either one of us any good."

She braced herself for the disclaimer that she knew would follow. And it did.

"However," he added firmly, "that doesn't change the fact that I'm here—I'm in this marriage—for our children." He caught her gaze. "We're clear on that?"

"Yes." For now maybe. But eventually he would come around. She knew he would. He simply had to. They had taken a huge step last night. Whether he wanted to admit it or not. Before the fight he'd been so close to falling in love. They could get there again. She would just have to be patient.

"That said, there's no reason why we shouldn't try to make the best of it."

"I have been," she reminded him.

"I know. And I've been selfish. But things will be different this time. I promise."

She wanted to believe him. She *had* to.

One of the babies rolled and started kicking her, and she automatically put a hand to her belly.

"Kicking?" he asked.

"Want to feel? You haven't in a long time." Not since the fight.

"I feel them every night. As soon as you go to sleep, they're all over the place. It amazes me that you can sleep through it."

She'd had no idea that he did that, that he felt his children moving inside her while she slept. That had to mean something, right?

He rolled onto his side next to her and laid a hand on her belly.

"We still have to talk about names," she said, watching her skin undulate with kicks and punches. "I was hoping we could use James. For my father."

"We could do that," he said, stroking her belly lower, and maybe it was wrong, but she was starting to get turned-on. "I was thinking Victoria, after my grandmother."

"I like that name," she said, closing her eyes, savoring the sensation of his hands on her skin. Then he slipped his hand between her legs, stroking her. It felt so good a moan worked its way up and past her lips.

"Wet already?" he asked, filling her with his fingers, and she gasped, arching to take them deeper. "I could make you come right now," he said, flicking her nipple with his tongue, causing that deep tug of pleasure in her womb. He could, but she hoped he wouldn't. She wanted to make this last, just in case for some reason, it might be the last time. She wanted to savor every second.

She tugged his towel open and his erection sprang up, so she leaned over and took him into her mouth. Sam groaned and tangled his fingers through her hair, letting his head fall back against the pillow. She knew exactly what to do to set him off, too. The perfect rhythm, the sensitive spot just below his testicles that she knew made him crazy. But when she could feel him getting close, his body tensing, he stopped her. He pushed her onto her back instead and climbed over her. He took her legs and hooked them, one over each of his shoulders, then he thrust inside her. Morning sex was usually slow and tranquil, but this was different. This was hot and sexy and...wild. In no time she was shuddering with release, but he didn't let himself have pleasure, wouldn't give in until she'd climaxed a second time. Would he be so concerned with her pleasure if he didn't care about her? Didn't *love* her?

She could drive herself crazy questioning his motives, so instead she cleared her mind, closed her eyes and just let herself feel.

Afterward Sam collapsed beside her, his chest heaving with the effort to catch his breath. "Bloody hell... that was...fantastic."

She lay on her back beside him, limp, her body buzzing with afterglow. "You probably noticed that my stomach is starting to get in the way."

"I did." He looked over at her and grinned. "Maybe next time we'll have to try it on our hands and knees."

She was going to suggest they try it right now, but then he looked at the time on his phone and cursed.

"You've made me late."

"Don't blame me. You started it."

"Yes, but if you weren't so irresistible, I wouldn't have been tempted."

Two days ago he wouldn't touch her, now she was irresistible? This was just too odd. But she wasn't about to complain. She felt as though she finally had her husband back. The emotional switch had been flipped back on. Now if she could only manage to keep it on, or even *find* the damned switch in the first place, everyone could be happy.

"I have to get ready," he said, pressing a kiss to her forehead before he rolled out of bed.

She listened to the sounds of him getting ready for work, as she had dozens of times before.

Like magic, Sam was back to his old self. He talked to her, teased her and spent time with her. And the sex? Good Lord, it had never been so fantastic. Or frequent. It was as though, despite how many times they made love, he simply couldn't get enough of her. It was a much needed salve to her ego, and at the same time, confused the hell out of her.

He had been quite clear in saying that he was only there for the children, yet he treated their relationship, their marriage, like the real thing. He had done a complete one-eighty, as if the weeks of misery had never happened. Or maybe it had been a terrible nightmare that she had finally woken up from. Whatever the reason, he was back to being the sweet, patient man she had married.

It was all she had ever hoped for, so she should be blissfully happy. Hell, she should be jumping with joy. Instead she was a nervous wreck, walking on eggshells. She was terrified that if she let her guard down she might say or do the wrong thing, and he would fall off the deep end again. Shut her out of his life.

She began to feel there was something wrong with her. Why couldn't she just relax and let herself be happy?

Maybe she really was the family screwup. Maybe she was destined to live her life in perpetual dysfunction. Or was it just that she was afraid the happier she let herself feel, the more it would hurt when the other shoe finally dropped?

Since their wedding, Anne had only seen Sam's parents a couple of times. And that was before their fight. Every time he had gone there since, he had some excuse why he couldn't take her. Although most times he didn't even bother to tell her he was going. She would find out later. It was almost as if he was sheltering them from her, maybe so they wouldn't get attached, and it made her feel terrible. She didn't want them to think that she was avoiding them, or even worse, didn't like them. She wanted a good relationship with her in-laws.

Finally, when they asked her and Sam to dinner one evening in late November, either he had run out of excuses, or he actually wanted her there, because he accepted. But then she found she was nervous. What had he told them about their marriage?

"Do they know?" Anne asked him as they were getting ready to leave, after she had obsessed for an hour about what to wear, trying on a dozen different outfits before she settled on a simple slip dress.

"Know what?" Sam asked.

"About us. How things have been." She hated mentioning it, reminding him—as if he would ever forget.

"I never said anything about it to them," he told her, holding her coat so she could slip it on. "As far as they know, everything is fine. And as far as I'm concerned, everything is."

She wished she could be so confident.

It had begun snowing that morning, the first of the

season, and by the time she and Sam got to his parents' house, a Tudor-style mansion, several inches had fallen, making the roads a bit treacherous.

The first thing his mother did, after they shed their boots and coats and gloves, was take Anne upstairs to show her the nursery and playroom they had already begun to set up for the twins.

"It's beautiful!" Anne told her, running her hand along the rail of one of the cribs. There were two. One with boy bedding and one for a girl. The walls were painted a gender-neutral shade of green, and there were shelves overflowing with toys and books. Many, she told Anne, used to be Sam's and Adam's.

"I haven't even started setting up the nursery," Anne told her. "Once Chris and Melissa move into the master suite, we'll be taking their old room, since the current nursery is right beside it."

"I hope you don't mind that we have a nursery," his mother said.

"Of course not."

"We know that as new parents it will be nice to occasionally have some time to yourselves. We would love to have the twins spend the night here every now and then. But we don't want to overstep our bounds."

"They're your grandchildren. Of course they can stay here."

She looked relieved. "I'm so glad. We weren't sure how you felt."

Because Anne was so absent from their lives. Her mother-in-law didn't say it, but Anne knew that was what she was thinking. And what could Anne say? *"It's not my fault. Your son has been keeping me from you."*

Then she would have to admit they had been having problems, and her mother-in-law would want to know why. Anne would be too humiliated to tell her what she had done to their son. The way she had lied to Sam. They would probably draw the same conclusion he had. They would think she was spoiled and selfish. That she had trapped him.

From now on, she would make an effort to spend more time with her in-laws. She would ask her mother-in-law to tea, or maybe they could go shopping in Paris or Milan. And she could invite them both to dinner at the castle.

"I'm sorry I don't make it over more," Anne said guiltily. "I feel I haven't been a very good daughter-in-law."

"Oh, Anne," she said, touching her arm. "Please, there's no need to apologize. Sam has explained how complicated it is for you with security and such. He said that you and your family are practically prisoners in the castle."

That was true, but it wasn't the reason for her absence. Sam had flat-out lied to his parents, and she couldn't help but think bitterly that dishonesty seemed to be okay if it suited his own needs, but if she wasn't completely candid all the time, it was wrong somehow. Talk about a double-edged sword and she was getting really tired of falling on it.

"I'll be so relieved when the man harassing you is caught," her mother-in-law said. "They should lock him up and throw away the key."

It was odd, but since they learned he was Geoffrey's son, and that he was emotionally disturbed, the profound hatred and resentment she felt before had fizzled out. Instead she felt deeply sorry for him. Not that she didn't want to see him locked up, but only so he could get the help he needed. She could only imagine the horrors he'd experienced in the military. Then to be refused help. It was unconscionable.

"He's a disturbed man who needs psychiatric help," Anne said. "Everyone will be relieved when he's caught."

Sam's father appeared in the doorway. "I thought I would find you two in here. Supper is ready."

She was probably being paranoid, but all through dinner Anne had the feeling that something was up. Sam's parents seemed...anxious. They picked at their food, a traditional English stew that was so delicious Anne actually had seconds. After dessert, they moved to the living room for brandy, or in Anne's case, mineral water. After they were all served, and the maid out of the room, Sam asked his parents, "So, are we going to talk about whatever it is that's bothering the two of you?"

Apparently Anne hadn't been the only one who noticed something was off.

"There is something we need to tell you," his father said, and his wife took his hand.

Anne had a feeling it wasn't going to be good news, and Sam must have shared her impression, because he frowned and asked, "What's wrong?"

"I went for my annual physical a few weeks ago and the doctor discovered that I have an enlarged prostate. They did some tests and they've come back positive for cancer. However," he added swiftly, "I'm in the early stages and he says it's one of the less aggressive types."

"He's not even recommending surgery," his mother said. "He thinks that with a round of radiation your father will be as good as new."

She could feel Sam's relief all but leaking from his pores as he sagged into the sofa beside her. "That's great. It could be much worse, right?"

"*Much* worse."

Sam looked from one parent to the other. "But there's something else, isn't there?"

They exchanged a look, then his father said. "I've decided that, for the sake of my health, it's time that I retire."

"Retire? But you love being prime minister. What will you do?"

"Relax, for a change. The truth is I've grown weary of politics. The long hours and constant conflict. I'm tired of it. I'm stepping down, and until my term ends six months from now, the deputy prime minister will take my place."

The change in Sam's stature was subtle, but Anne felt it right away, and she knew exactly what he was thinking. If it weren't for his marriage, for *her,* Sam would be running to take his father's place. And he would get it, because out of anyone else who might choose to run, he would be the most qualified. He would be prime minister, just as he had always wanted.

But now that was never going to happen. And it was all her fault.

Maybe she imagined it, but she swore she could feel

that emotional switch snap off. And all she could think was, *Oh God, here we go again.*

"I suppose he'll run for your seat after that," Sam said.

"I'm sure he will," his father said, and Anne knew just what Sam was thinking. He had declared more than once that the deputy was a moron.

"I know this will be difficult for you, son," his father said, avoiding Anne's gaze.

"I'm fine," Sam told him, forcing a smile. Another lie. "You shouldn't even be worrying about how his will affect me. All that matters right now is your health. If you're happy, I'm happy for you."

He sounded sincere, but Anne knew better, and in the back of her mind she heard the distinct clunk of that pesky other shoe dropping.

Since the weather was getting progressively worse, they left his parents' house a short time later. Only when they were in the car and on their way back to the castle did Sam let down his guard, and she saw how truly upset he was.

"The deputy is a wanker," he said.

But he was handsome and congenial, and people had been elected on far less.

"Sam," she started to say, but he held up a hand to hush her.

"Please, don't. Not now."

She knew this was going to happen. That it was inevitable. She'd felt it in her bones. Unfortunately, that didn't make the reality of the situation any easier to accept. Although in a very strange way, it was a relief to finally have it over with.

She leaned back against the seat and looked out into the night, watching as fat snowflakes drifted past the car window. She tried to tell herself that this was just a small blip, and in a day or two, everything would be okay.

She told herself that, because the alternative was unimaginable. If he shut her out again, how long would it take this time to drag him back out of his shell?

And this time, did she even want to try?

Twelve

He knew it was selfish and unfair, but Sam couldn't even look at Anne.

The idea of never following in his father's footsteps had been upsetting, but easier to stomach when the prospect seemed so far in the future. Now here it was staring him right in the face. He was forced once again to rehash everything he'd lost. Everything he wanted and would never have. And he blamed her.

On top of that his father had cancer. Sam could only hope he was being honest about the prognosis, and not sugarcoating the truth so Sam wouldn't worry.

With the inclement weather it took twice the normal time to get home. And he used the term "home" loosely, because right now he felt as if he were in limbo. One foot in and one out of his marriage. His life. He needed some time to himself, to work things through and regroup. If there was any possible way he could justify not staying at the castle for a day or two, he would be gone. The construction on his town house had been completed months ago, so he could stay there. But then there was the problem of her family. If he wasn't careful, he would find himself miserable *and* unemployed. At least with a job he enjoyed, he had someplace to escape to.

Otherwise, he was trapped.

Anne was quiet while they got ready for bed, but when they climbed under the covers, she reached for him. Though he felt like a bastard for it, he shrugged away from her. She was only trying to comfort him, trying to be a good wife, but he couldn't let her in. Not yet. The wound was still too fresh.

It'll be better tomorrow, he assured himself. But the next morning, after a long night of tossing and turning, he only felt worse. Anne tried to talk to him, but he shook his head and told her, "I'm not ready," hating himself for the hurt look she didn't bother trying to hide. He wasn't being fair—there had to come a time when he forgave her and moved on—but he couldn't help the way he felt. The bitterness and resentment. He kept telling himself, tomorrow it will better. But it wasn't. Every day that passed he pulled deeper inside his shell.

Only days ago he had been close to forgiving her—to putting it all behind them. Now he felt as though he would be angry with her indefinitely.

It was killing Anne to see Sam so unhappy.

She had hoped that by now he would have come around, but since his father's announcement two weeks ago they had been in a steady free fall. She had tried to be patient and sympathetic. She tried to give him space to work things through. And still he kept telling her that he needed time. She just wasn't sure if she had any left to give.

He was miserable, and she was miserable, and though she loved him, she simply didn't have the strength to fight anymore. Not when it was a one-sided battle. And forcing him to stay with her, when he clearly didn't want to be there, wasn't right. It wasn't fair to him, or her, or even the babies.

She wasn't a quitter, and she had tried damned hard to make it work, but this was a losing battle. She could no longer take his Jekyll and Hyde mood swings. And even if he did come around again, how could she be sure that the next time things got hard, he wouldn't do this again? And again. She couldn't live like this anymore, always on her guard. Waiting for the next disaster.

It was clear that the only way they would ever be happy again was if they were apart. For good.

Making that final decision had been hard, but at the same time a huge burden had been lifted. She felt…free. The really tough part was going to Chris and admitting that, after only a few months, her marriage was over.

"I had the feeling something was wrong," he told her. "But I had hoped you would work it out."

"We tried," she said. Or at least, *she* had. But this whole mess was her fault in the first place, so it didn't seem fair to blame only him. "It just isn't going to work. We're miserable."

"So what you're saying is, you want permission to divorce."

"I understand the position I'm putting the family in and I'm sorry."

He sighed. "A little scandal won't kill us."

"So you'll allow it?"

"If there's one thing we've learned, it's that life is short. You deserve to be happy, not chained to a marriage that isn't working. I can't deny that I'm very fond of Sam. He's done one hell of a job as ambassador."

"But after the divorce, he'll be able to go back to politics. Right?"

"He'll be stripped of his title, so yes, he can hold any office he wants."

Well, she could give him that at least. And telling Chris made it feel so much more... *final.* She had to fight not to give in to her grief, reach deep inside herself to find the old Anne. *The Shrew.* The Anne who didn't need anyone, or care what anyone thought of her. And still, somewhere deep down, she couldn't help but cling to the slender hope that when faced with the real prospect of their marriage ending, Sam would suddenly comprehend everything he was giving up. Maybe he would even realize that he loved her.

She waited until that evening to approach him. He had just come home from work and was in their room changing for dinner. She walked in and shut the door behind her.

"We need to talk," she said.

Without even glancing her way he said, "Now isn't a good time."

"Then I'll talk and you can just listen."

He turned to her, looking pained, and she almost felt

sorry for him. He was miserable and he was doing it to himself. "I'm not ready. I need time."

"Well, I can't do this anymore," she said.

"Do what?"

"This. *Us.* We're both unhappy. I think it would be best…" The words caught in her throat. *Come on, Anne, hold it together.* She squared her shoulders. "I think it would best for everyone if we called it quits."

He narrowed his eyes at her, as though he thought it might be a trick. After a pause he asked, "Is this the part where I have a change of heart and realize I can't live without you?"

Apparently not. She swallowed back the sorrow rising up from deep inside her. This was it. It was really the end. Her marriage was over. "No. This is the part where I ask you to leave, and tell you I want a divorce."

He just stood there, like he was waiting for the punch line. When it didn't come he said, "You're serious."

She nodded.

"So that's it? Just like that, it's over?"

She shrugged, tried to pretend she wasn't coming apart on the inside. "Just like that."

"You're just giving up?"

"It takes two people to make a marriage work, Sam. You gave up a long time ago. And I can't fight for this anymore."

He didn't deny it, because he knew she was right.

"I've already talked to my attorney and he's drawing up the divorce papers immediately."

"You said before that once we're married, that's it."

"I talked to Chris and he's going to allow it. And he assured me that the second it's legal you will be stripped of your title. That should give you plenty of time to set up a campaign and run for prime minister. You'll have everything you've ever wanted."

He still looked hesitant. Honestly, she thought he'd have been packing by now.

"Why are you doing this?" he asked. "Why now?"

"Because I can't live like this anymore. I may have made a terrible mistake, Sam, but I can't pay for it for the rest of my life. I deserve to be happy. To be married to someone who loves me, not a man who tolerates me for the sake of our children."

"I married you for their sake."

Yes, he had, and shame on her for forgetting that. "There's no benefit to their parents being married if everyone is miserable. We'll share custody, and they will grow up knowing both their parents love them very much, even if they don't live in the same household. They'll live perfectly happy lives, like millions of other kids whose parents are divorced."

"And my ambassadorship?"

"Chris is arranging for a replacement as we speak. You are free to pursue a job you actually like. Effective immediately."

"I did like my job," he said.

"But now you can have the one you want."

He was quiet for a long time, as though he was working it through. Processing it. She started to feel the faintest glimmer of hope. Maybe he was beginning to realize what he was about to lose.

But then he nodded and said, "It probably is for the best." Driving the proverbial stake through her heart.

If he loved her, even a little bit, he would want to fight for her.

"I'd like you gone tonight," she said, struggling to maintain her composure. To keep her voice even, her expression cold.

She was *The Shrew*, she reminded herself. She didn't let people hurt her.

"If that's what you want," he said.

No, she wanted to shout. She wanted *him,* the way he had been right after their wedding. The man who had been so sweet and caring when she lost her father. Her *partner.*

She wanted him to love her. But that was never going to happen.

"It's what I want. I'll go so you can pack."

"You're sure about this?"

"I've never been so sure of anything in my life. I just…" She swallowed hard. "I just don't love you anymore."

"It was never about love."

Not for him maybe, but it had been for her. And saying she didn't love him now was a lie.

But this was one lie she was sure he could live with.

Sam was relieved.

He was out of a job, a signature away from divorce, and wouldn't live in the same house as his twin infants. And he was happy about it.

At least, that's what he had been telling himself. Over and over. And he was sure, in time, he might actually start believing it.

He moved back into his town house, with its shiny new kitchen and sagless ceilings. Exactly where he had wanted to be. Only to realize that it didn't much feel like home anymore.

It would just take time to adjust, he kept telling himself. He could get on with his life now. He could follow in his father's footsteps and run for the prime minister's seat. Even though the mere idea of an arduous campaign exhausted him. He hadn't even thought about whom he would hire to run it, much less a platform to run on.

But he had made the right decision, leaving Anne—of course, he hadn't left so much as been kicked out.

And if he was so sure then why, after three days of moping, hadn't he told his parents? It was only a matter of time before the story made it to the press. He couldn't abide by them reading in the newspaper that their son had failed at being a husband.

And that was how he felt. Like a complete failure.

But he couldn't put it off any longer.

"What a nice surprise!" his father said, when Sam popped in unannounced. But as he shrugged out of his coat and handed it to the maid, his father frowned. "Have you been sick?"

"What makes you ask that?"

"Well, it's Wednesday. You're not at work. And forgive me for saying so, but you look terrible."

He must have been a sight with tousled hair and several days' worth of beard stubble. Not to mention his wrinkled clothes. He hadn't unpacked yet and had been living out of a suitcase and boxes. "No, I'm not sick. But I do need to talk to you about something."

"How about a drink?" his father offered.

Figuring he would need the liquid courage, Sam said, "Make it a double."

While he poured, Sam asked, "Is Mom around?"

"She had some luncheon to attend." He shrugged. "One of her charities, I think. I lose track."

He had hoped to tell them both together, but since he was already here… Besides, it might be easier talking to his father first.

He handed Sam his drink. "Shall we sit in the den?"

"Sure." He followed his father down the hall, thinking how, in all the years they had lived there, not much had changed. But Sam had. And he would be the first to admit he was very fond of the familiar. He was a creature of habit, so change made him…edgy. And right now, his entire life felt turned upside down.

When they were seated in the den, Sam on the sofa and his father in his favorite chair, he asked, "So, what's up?"

Sam sat on the edge of the cushion, elbows resting on his knees, swirling the scotch in his glass. "I thought you should know that I moved out of the castle last week. Anne and I are getting a divorce."

"I'm sorry to hear that, Sam. You two seemed so happy."

They were. For a while. Until things got so complicated.

"Can I ask what happened?"

Sam considered telling him the truth. About the night of the twins' conception and the fact that Anne had lied about birth control. Then continued to lie even after they were married. But he realized that really had nothing to do with this.

So, she had made a mistake. Yes, he'd been angry, and he'd felt betrayed. And he'd struggled so damned hard to hold on to to it, to…punish her. When he finally let go, let himself forgive her, it had been a relief.

This was different. This wasn't about what she had done, although at first it had been easier to blame her than to admit what was really bothering him. Because that was the way he liked things. Easy.

But really, he'd only made things more complicated.

"I screwed up," he told his father, taking a long swallow of his drink, but the path of fire it scored in his throat didn't come close to the burning ache in his heart. "I screwed up and I don't know how to fix it. If it even is fixable."

"Do you love her?"

It surprised him how quickly the answer surfaced. "Yeah. I do."

"Have you told her that?"

No. In fact, he'd told her specifically that he *didn't* love her. That he never would. That he was only in it for the kids. "It wasn't supposed to be about love. That wasn't part of the plan."

His father laughed. "In my experience, son, things rarely go as planned. Especially when it comes to love."

Yes, but if it wasn't about love, then it would be easy. No messy emotions to get in the way and complicate things. It was when he started falling in love with her that everything got so confusing.

He downed the last of his drink and set the empty glass on the coffee table. "It shouldn't be this complicated."

"What?"

"Relationships. Marriage. It shouldn't be this hard."

"If it were easy, don't you think it would get... boring?"

"Is it too much to want what you and Mom have?"

"And what do we have?"

"The perfect marriage. You never fought or had problems. It was so *easy* for you. It just...worked."

"Sam, our marriage is *far* from perfect."

"Okay, I know you two have had your little spats, but—"

"Infidelity? Do you consider that a little spat?"

At first he thought his father was kidding, and when he saw that he was, in fact, *very* serious, Sam's jaw dropped. "You cheated on Mom?"

He shook his head solemnly. "Never. I've never once been unfaithful to your mother. Not that I didn't have the opportunity. But I loved her too much. Too much for my own good."

"If you didn't—" The meaning of his father's words suddenly sank in and they almost knocked him backward. "Are you saying that *Mom* was unfaithful to *you?*"

"You remember how much she toured, all the attention she got. Not to mention that she's an incredibly beautiful woman."

Sam could hardly believe what he was hearing. *"When?"*

"You were eight."

"I—I'm *stunned*. I had no idea."

"And we never meant for you to find out. Now I'm beginning to think that sheltering you from the realities of our relationship was a mistake. Marriages take work, son. They're complicated and messy."

"What did you do when you found out?"

"I was devastated. And I seriously considered leaving. I went so far as to pack my bags, but she begged me to forgive her, to give her a second chance. We decided together that we would go to counseling and try to save our marriage. She even took a year off from touring, to prove to me that she was serious. That our relationship came first."

"I remember that," Sam said. "I remember her being home all the time. I just never stopped to think why, I guess."

"Why would you? You were a little boy. And always so happy. So bright and cheerful. We didn't want our problems to reflect negatively on you. Or Adam. Although I think he suspected."

"How could you ever trust her again?"

"It wasn't easy. Especially after she went back to touring. We had a few very rough years. But I think our marriage is better for it. If we could survive that, we can survive almost anything."

Sam felt as if his entire world had been flipped on its axis. His parents' perfect marriage hadn't been perfect at all. He had been holding himself, his own marriage, to such a ridiculously high standard that the instant they hit a snag, he'd felt like a failure, that he wasn't measuring up. He had expected Anne to conform to some cardboard cut-out version of his perfect mother, never knowing that person didn't even exist.

He pinched the bridge of his nose. "I. Am. A *wanker.*"

His dad grinned. "You can't learn if you don't make mistakes."

"Well, I've made a monumental one. All of the troubles Anne and I have been having revolve around one thing, my desire to run for the prime minister's seat. And I've been so damned busy focusing on what I can't have, instead of what I do have, I've completely overlooked the fact that I don't want to be prime minister anymore."

When his father announced his retirement, it had been the perfect excuse to push Anne away. So he wouldn't have to admit that he was falling in love with her.

"Are you disappointed?" he asked his father.

He looked puzzled. "Why would I be disappointed?"

"Well, I always planned to follow in your footsteps."

"Sam, you have to walk your own path, make your own footprint. You have to do what makes *you* happy."

"I'm happy as an ambassador. And I'm damned good at it. Or at least, I *was.*"

"They fired you?"

He shrugged. "Anne, the job, it was a package deal." And he had blown it.

His entire life Sam had known exactly what he wanted, and he had never been afraid of anything. But now he wasn't just afraid. He was terrified. Terrified that it was too late.

"Do you want her back?" his father asked.

"More than anything. But I'm not so sure she'll give me another chance. Or if I even deserve one."

"Can I give you a bit of advice?"

Sam nodded.

"The most precious things in life are the ones you have to fight for. So ask yourself, is she worth fighting for?"

He didn't even have to think about it. "Yes, she is."

"So what are you going to do?"

There was only one thing he could do. "I guess I'm going to fight."

Thirteen

Sam headed back to his town house to shower and change before he went to see Anne, only to be met at the front door and served with an envelope containing the divorce papers.

He didn't bother to open it, since he had no intention of signing them. But it was clear, when he got to the castle, that she wasn't going to make this reconciliation easy for him.

"I'm sorry, sir," the guard posted at the gate said, when Sam pulled up. "I can't let you in."

"It's very important," Sam told him, but the man didn't budge. "Come on, you *know* me."

When he was part of the family, the guard's expression said. "I do apologize, sir. But I have strict orders not to let you in."

He said he would fight for her, and that was what he

planned to do, even to the detriment of his pride. "Can you just call up and tell her I'm here?"

"Sir—"

"Please, just do me this favor. Call her and tell her that I *need* to see her."

He hesitated, then stepped back into his booth and picked up the phone. Sam breathed a sigh of relief. If Anne knew he was out here waiting, that he needed to talk to her, surely she would let him in.

The guard spoke into the phone, nodded a few times, then hung up. Sam waited for him to reach for the lever that would open the gate and wave him past. Instead, he stepped back out of the booth and over to Sam's car window. "If you require an audience with the princess, it was suggested that you contact her personal assistant or the palace social secretary."

Now she was being ridiculous. They were still *married* for God's sake. And had she forgotten that she was pregnant with *his* children?

He pulled out his cell phone and dialed her private number. It rang three times, then went to voice mail. He tried her cell phone next. This time it went straight to voice mail. He listened to the generic message, and after the tone said, "Anne, this is ridiculous. Pick up the phone."

He disconnected, then immediately dialed again. Again, he got her voice mail. Either she was rejecting his calls, or the phone was off, but he knew that she always kept her phone on, so he was guessing it was the latter.

He texted her a message: CALL ME!!!!!!

He waited, but after a moment she hadn't replied, and his phone wasn't ringing.

"Sir," the guard said firmly. "I'm going to have to ask you to leave."

"Hold on."

He tried Louisa's phone with no luck, then Melissa's, then as a last-ditch effort, he called Chris's office line, but his secretary fed him some garbage about His Highness being out of the office.

He was being stonewalled.

He texted her again: I'm not giving up. I'm going to fight for you.

"Mr. Baldwin." A second, more threatening-looking guard with a holstered sidearm appeared at his window. "I'm going to have to insist that you leave right now."

Sam could insist that he was staying, and demand to see Anne, but it would most likely land him in jail. He could try to sneak onto the grounds, but with Richard Corrigan still at large, Sam would no doubt be shot on sight.

"All right, I'm going," he grumbled.

She'd completely shut him out. And hadn't he done the exact same thing to her? Hadn't he shut her out emotionally?

He couldn't help thinking that he was getting a taste of his own medicine. That didn't mean he had any intention of giving up.

She had told him she was tired of being the only one fighting to save their marriage. Well, if it was a fight she wanted, that was what she was about to get.

"Sam again?" Louisa asked, when Anne's cell rang for the *bazillionth* time that morning. They were in

Louisa's room, on the Internet, registering for baby things in preparation for Anne's shower in January.

"Who else?" Anne grabbed it and rejected the call. He had been calling and texting and e-mailing incessantly. "I'm going to have to change my bloody number. And my e-mail address."

Louisa bit her lip.

"What?" Anne said.

She pasted on an innocent look and said, "I didn't say a word."

"No, but you want to. I can tell."

Louisa had seen Sam leave with his suitcases that night a week ago—although it felt more like a month—and Anne had finally broken down and told her everything that happened.

"It's just that he's very...persistent," Louisa said gently. "Maybe you should talk to him."

According to his numerous texts—which Anne had grudgingly read but refused to answer—and all the messages he had left on her phone, he loved her, and he wanted to fight to make their marriage work. But she didn't have any fight left in her.

"I have nothing left to say to him."

"You're having his babies, Annie. You can't ignore him forever."

She didn't plan to. She would talk to him eventually, but not until she felt it was safe. Not until she woke in the morning without that sick, empty feeling in her heart, until she could go more than five minutes without seeing his face or hearing his voice in her head. Not until she could face him and not long to throw herself into his arms and hold him.

She needed time to get over him.

Her phone buzzed as a text came through.

I'm not giving up. I love you.

Apparently he'd forgotten that this wasn't about love. Besides, he didn't really love her. He just didn't like losing. But this time he wouldn't charm his way back into her heart. Not when she knew he would only break it again.

"You know I love you, Annie, and I'm always on your side…" Louisa began.

"But?"

"Don't you think you're being just a little…unfair?"

"Unfair? Was Sam being fair when he ignored me for *weeks?"*

"So you're getting revenge? Giving him a taste of his own medicine?"

"No! That's not what I meant."

"Just call him. Tell him it's over."

"I did tell him. The night I kicked him out."

"Well, apparently the message didn't get through, and until you level with him, he's going to keep thinking there's hope. I don't have to tell you what that's like."

She hated that Louisa's words made so much sense.

Her phone started ringing again. Louisa picked it up and handed it to her. "Talk to him. If not for yourself, then do it for me."

She hesitated, then took the phone and Louisa walked out, leaving her alone. She took a deep breath, terrified that when she heard his voice, she was going to melt.

You are *The Shrew,* she reminded herself. A cold-hearted bitch who doesn't need anyone.

Now, if she could just make herself believe it.

* * *

Anne had ignored so many of his calls that when she finally did answer, he forgot what he was going to say. But that wasn't a problem, because she didn't give him a chance to say a word.

"I only accepted your call to ask you to please stop bothering me. I don't want to talk to you."

"Then I'll do the talking and you can listen."

"Sam—"

"I am so sorry for the way I treated you. I love you, Annie."

"It's not supposed to be about love," she said, throwing his words back in his face. Not that he blamed her.

"I know, but I fell in love with you anyway. And it scared the hell out of me."

"Why?"

"I thought that loving you would be too hard. Turns out, loving you was the easy part. The hard part was pushing you away."

"I can't be with someone who flakes out on me every time things get hard. Every time I make a mistake."

"I know my track record up until now hasn't been great, and I'm sorry, but if you give me another chance, I swear it will be different this time."

"That's what you said the last time."

"This time I mean it."

"I want to believe you. I truly do. But I just can't take the chance. The way things were, I just…I can't do that again."

"Annie—"

"It's over, Sam. Please don't call me again."

The line went dead, and Sam stared dumbfounded at the phone.

She was turning him down?

And why shouldn't she? Why should she believe a word he said? Had he just assumed, after the way he had treated her, that he could simply pour his heart out and she would beg him to come home?

A part of him wanted to be angry. He wanted to believe that she was only doing this to be stubborn. To get revenge. But that wasn't Anne's style. She'd loved him, and she had done everything she could to try to make their marriage work. She stuck by him, even when he was treating her like a pariah. And what thanks had she gotten? Absolutely none. He hadn't been the least bit grateful. He hadn't even *tried* to make it work.

The truth was, he didn't deserve her. And maybe they would both be better off if he just let her go.

Anne's feet were swollen and sore and her back ached something special, so the last place she wanted to be was standing out in the freezing cold in front of a crowd of doctors, nurses and television media. But Melissa was in the throes of twenty-four-hour morning sickness, so Chris asked Anne to accompany him to the ground-breaking ceremony for the new pediatric cancer center at the hospital.

They stood on the platform, in the brisk wind, waiting for the hospital administrator to finish his spiel. She kept her hands tucked in her coat pockets, probably looking to everyone like she was just trying to stay warm, when in fact, she clutched her cell phone in her right hand, waiting to feel the buzz alerting her to an incoming call or text message. But as it had been the past two weeks, it remained stubbornly silent.

There had to be something wrong with her. For days Sam had called nonstop and all she had wanted was for him to leave her alone, but now that he had, she longed to hear his voice.

She kept thinking about what he'd said the last time they talked, wondering if he actually meant it this time. He'd told her that he loved her and she was starting to believe him. But she was still too afraid to accept it, to face the possibility that he might just hurt her all over again.

But if he called, if *he* made the first move…again. Why would he when she had asked him to leave her alone? But if he loved her, would he really give up that easily? And was she forgetting all the texts and phone calls that she had refused to answer?

She shivered and hunched her shoulders against a sudden burst of icy wind.

"Whose brilliant idea was it to do this in December?" she grumbled under her breath.

"It's almost over," Chris assured her softly. "Just hang in there."

She glanced over at him, irritable and cold, and wanting to do something really childish, like stick her tongue out at him. She did a swift double take when she noticed a tiny red spot on the lapel of his coat. Had that been there earlier? At first she figured it was some sort of stain, or a stray fleck of lint. Then it moved.

What the—?

She was sure her eyes were playing tricks on her, then the spot moved again, from his lapel to the left side of his chest. It was a light, she realized, like a laser pointer—

It hit her then, what it could be, and her heart clenched. She knew there was no time to alert Gunter, who stood behind her. She had to do something. Now.

Time screeched to a halt, then picked up in slow motion, the seconds ticking by like hours as she yanked her hands free from her pockets and reached up, shoving Chris as hard as she could. She saw his stunned expression the same instant she felt her arm jerked back painfully, and felt herself being pulled over. She braced for the pain of the hard platform as she landed, but instead she landed on a person. Gunter, she realized. He rolled her over to her side away from the crowd and shielded her with his enormous body. Then someone shouted for a medic and her heart froze. Had she been too late? Had Chris been hit?

She tried to push up on her elbow, to see him, and Gunter ordered, "Stay down!"

She lay there helpless, imagining her brother bleeding to death only a few inches away. Her ears began to ring, all but drowning out the frightened screams of the people fleeing the area.

Then everything went black.

Sam sat slumped on the couch in his town house, nursing a scotch and brooding. Or sulking. Or a combination of the two.

His cell had been ringing almost constantly for two hours, but none of the calls were from Anne and he didn't feel like talking to anyone. Not when he was perfectly content to sit here alone and contemplate the fact that he'd had everything a man could hope for and he had callously thrown it away.

The divorce papers lay on the coffee table in front of him, still unsigned. He just couldn't seem to make himself pick up a pen. He didn't want a divorce. Didn't want to lose Anne.

But she wanted to lose him and hadn't he put her through enough grief? Didn't he owe it to her to set her free? Even though the idea of her falling in love with someone else and some other man raising his children made him physically ill. But he knew Anne well enough to realize that refusing a divorce wouldn't stop her from getting on with her life. She was so stubborn, it would probably make her that much more determined to forget him.

He sat up and grabbed the document. He hadn't read it, but his lawyer assured him it was pretty cut-and-dry. They would both leave the marriage with exactly what they had brought to it. It would almost be as if it had never happened.

He flipped to the page that was flagged for him to sign. He could *do* this. He grabbed the pen off the table, took a deep breath, raised the pen to the paper…and his damned phone started ringing again.

"Bloody hell!" He snatched the phone up off the table, flipped it open and barked, "What do you want?"

"Sam?" his brother, Adam, asked, clearly taken aback.

"Yes, it's me. It's my phone you called."

"Where have you been? We've been trying to reach you for an hour."

"I'm home. And the fact that I haven't answered should tell you that I don't feel like talking to anyone."

"I thought you would have been at the hospital by now."

"Why would I be at the hospital?" Did his brother think he was so depressed that he would be suicidal?

"You haven't heard the news?"

"What news?"

"There was a shooting. The king and Anne were outside the hospital for some ceremony and there was an assassination attempt."

Oh Jesus. He grabbed the remote and switched the television on. "Is Chris okay?"

"It was confirmed he wasn't hit. Anne shoved him out of the way at the last minute. She saved his life. But, Sam..."

Adam's words faded into the background as the banner announcing a "breaking story" flashed across the screen, and he saw the headline, *Assassination Attempt. Princess Anne Rushed to Hospital.* The remote slipped from his fingers and clattered to the floor and his heart slammed the wall of his chest so hard he couldn't draw in a full breath.

This was not happening.

He listened numbly as the newscaster relayed the events of the shooting. Then they ran a clip of the shooting taken by one of the television cameras in the crowd. Sam watched in disbelief as one minute Anne and Chris were just standing there listening to the hospital administrator, then Anne glanced up at her brother, and suddenly shoved him hard. Gunter was on her immediately, taking her down and out of the shooter's line of sight, then the camera's view was blocked by the podium. Sam couldn't tell if she'd been hit and when it cut back to the newscaster, she said there was still no word on the extent of the princess's injuries, only that she had been unconscious.

He didn't hear anything after that. What must have been a rush of adrenaline propelled him up off the couch. Only when he was on his feet and heading for the door, grabbing his keys and coat on the way out, did he realize he was still holding his phone and Adam was shouting his name.

"I'll call you back," he said, and disconnected. He needed to get to the hospital now.

This was *his* fault. He should have been there with her, standing by her side on that platform. And he would never forgive himself if she and the babies weren't okay.

Fourteen

If a person had to be shot at, what better place than right outside of a hospital?

Anne sat in bed, in the royal family's private wing, wearing one of those irritating, backless gowns that left her behind exposed. And she had no idea why she required a bare ass when all she had were a few minor bumps and bruises from Gunter pulling her down. They had admitted her only because she'd passed out, which embarrassed her terribly, and, even though she'd landed on Gunter, they worried the fall may have hurt the babies. And though everything was fine, they still insisted she should stay overnight for observation.

It was worth it to know that Chris was safe.

The police told her that if she hadn't pushed Chris aside, he would almost assuredly be dead.

Had she acted an instant later, he would have taken a

bullet to the chest, and if she'd reacted a second sooner, the bullet probably would have hit her head instead. Either Chris would be dead, or she would. The idea still gave her cold chills.

The best part was that the police had *finally* arrested Richard Corrigan. Apparently being on the run, and in hiding, had gotten to him. He hadn't even tried to get away this time. The plan had been to kill Chris and then himself, but the police got to him before he could carry out the second half.

Finally, this terrible nightmare, the harassment and threats, were over. They were free again.

As soon as the doctor would allow visitors, her family had flooded the room, needing to see with their own eyes that she was all right. Even though the doctor assured them she was doing exceptionally well for someone who was just shot at and pregnant with twins to boot.

Chris chastised her for putting her and the twins' lives in jeopardy for him, then he hugged her fiercely. She could swear she even saw the sheen of tears in his eyes.

She wanted to call Sam. The last thing she wanted was for him to see it on the news and think the worst, but her phone had gone missing in all the chaos. Everyone had been trying to reach him. Her family, and Gunter, and even the police, but apparently he wasn't answering his phone.

"I'm sure as soon as he hears he'll be here," her mother assured her. She had been sitting on the edge of the bed holding Anne's hand since they let the family in. Louisa was on the opposite side and both her brothers stood near the foot of the bed. There was nothing like a near-death experience to bring a family closer.

Everyone but Sam.

Maybe Sam had heard about the shooting but she had driven him so far away he just didn't care anymore.

She immediately shook the thought away, writing it off as utterly ridiculous. Even if he didn't care about her anymore, he still loved his children.

Gunter stepped into the room about fifteen minutes later and Anne looked to him hopefully, but he shook his head. "We send car, but he was not home."

"So where the heck *is* he?"

"He'll come," Louisa assured her.

"Could he have gone out of town?" Melissa asked, stepping up beside Chris.

"Or to his parents' house?" Liv suggested.

"We already tried there," Anne said.

As she was combing her mind, trying to imagine where else he could possibly be, the door flew open and Sam was there.

His eyes darted to the bed, and when he saw her sitting there, she could actually see him go weak with relief. She didn't have to ask her family to give them privacy. They were barely out the door before Sam had crossed the room and was holding her. The feel of his body, his familiar scent, nearly brought her to tears. How could she have even thought that letting go of him was a good thing?

"On the news all they said was that you might have been shot." He squeezed her, burying his face in her hair. "I didn't know if you were alive or dead. If I would ever see you again. Then I got here and the stupid people downstairs wouldn't tell me anything."

"Well, I'm not dead," she said, and he held her even tighter.

"You're okay? The babies are okay?"

"We're fine. I'm only in here because I passed out."

"I thought I lost you. For good this time." He cupped her face in his hands and kissed her. Firmly and prickly. Then he pulled away and she realized why. It had been so long since he'd shaved, he'd surpassed stubble and now had a full-fledged beard. His hair was shaggy, too, and in need of a trim. And she was guessing, by the dark smudges under his eyes, that he'd been sleeping as poorly as she had. And to top the look off, under his cashmere coat he wore a T-shirt and cartoon-emblazoned cotton pants.

He looked terrible. And wonderful.

"Nice pants," she said.

He looked down at himself and laughed, as though he'd just realized he'd left the house in his pajamas. And because she could, she reached up and touched his dimple.

"Suffice it to say I left in a hurry." He took her hand in his and kissed it. "Annie, I have been such an ass—"

She put a finger over his lips to shush him. "We *both* acted really stupid. But we're smarter now."

"Definitely." He kissed her fingers, her wrist. "I didn't sign the divorce papers. And I'm not going to. I flat-out refuse. I plan to spend the rest of my life with you."

"Good, because I didn't sign them, either. After you move back to the castle, we'll build a big fire in the study and watch them burn."

His eyes locked on hers. "And then we'll make love all night."

She sighed. That sounded wonderful.

He smiled, touched her face. "I am so proud of you."

"For what?"

"For *what?*" He laughed. "What do you think? You saved your brother's life. You're a hero."

"I wasn't trying to be. Everything happened so fast. I saw the laser sight on his coat and I just pushed him."

His brow furrowed. "I should have been there for you."

"But you're here now."

"I'm not leaving you again, Annie. I love you so much."

"I love you, too, Sam.

"I've said it before, but things will be different this time. I know, because *I'm* different."

"Me, too. There's nothing like a near-death experience to set your priorities straight."

He kissed her again, then said, "Scoot over."

He dropped his coat on the floor and crawled into bed beside her, drawing her close to his side. She had never felt more content, more happy in her life. And it was nice to know that she wasn't the family screwup after all. She could finally just relax and be happy.

"I have a confession to make," he said. "About the night of the charity ball. My friends dared me to ask you to dance. And I was tipsy enough to take the bait."

"And here I just thought you were exceedingly brave," she teased.

"You're not angry?"

"I think it's sort of funny, actually. Considering you got a whole lot more than just a dance."

"But you know what? I'm glad you lied to me that night. If it wasn't for the babies, I never would have had the guts to take a chance on myself." He kissed the tip of her nose. "On us. Because we're supposed to be together."

"I think I figured that out a long time ago."

He grinned. "You're clearly smarter than I am."

"I have a confession, too," she said. "And it's a little… well, *racy*, I guess."

One brow peaked with curiosity. "I'm all ears."

She slipped her hand under his shirt, laid it on his warm stomach. "I've always wondered what it would be like to fool around in a hospital bed."

His smile was a wicked one. "You don't say."

"But until now," she said, sliding her hand upward, to his chest. "I've never had the chance to test it out."

He must have had his hand right by the bed controls, because suddenly the head of the bed was sliding down. "I have an idea, Princess."

"Oh yeah? What's that?"

He lowered his head and kissed her, whispering against her lips, "Let's fool around and find out."

Epilogue

June

The babies were finally asleep.

Anne blew a silent kiss to her slumbering angels, made sure the baby monitor was on, then gathered the skirt of her gown and crept quietly from the nursery.

"I'll be back to check on them later," she told their nanny, Daria.

"Have a good time, Your Highness."

A glance up at the clock said she was already an hour late, but motherhood was her number one priority these days. Still, she didn't want to make him wait *too* long.

She stopped in her room to check her makeup one last time, then rushed down to the ballroom. In honor of her father, they were holding their second annual charity ball. And she could see, as she descended the stairs, that the turnout was even more impressive than last year.

Standing just inside the ballroom, chatting with Chris and Melissa, was Melissa's family, the royals of Morgan Isle. King Phillip and Queen Hannah, Prince Ethan and his wife, Lizzy, and the Duke, Charles Mead, and his wife, Victoria.

Several feet away Louisa and Princess Sophia stood, both pregnant and just beginning to show, comparing baby bumps while their husbands wore amused grins.

But the one person she wanted to see, who was supposedly waiting for her, was nowhere in sight.

Anne nabbed a glass of champagne from a passing waiter—the babies would be getting pumped milk tonight—sipped deeply and scanned the crowd.

"You're looking lovely, Your Highness," someone said from behind her.

The sound of his voice warmed her from the inside out.

She turned to face him. "A pleasure to see you again, Mr. Baldwin."

He bowed in greeting, and as he did a lock of that unruly blond hair fell across his forehead. "Please, call me Sam."

"Would you care to dance, Sam?"

He grinned, his dimples winking. The fire in his eyes still burned bright after a year. "I thought you'd never ask."

He took her hand and led her out to the dance floor, pulling her into his arms and holding her close. She pressed her cheek to his, breathed in the scent of his cologne.

"I'm the envy of every man in the room," he whispered.

She didn't know about that, but no one called her *The Shrew* any longer. That woman had ceased to exist the moment she met this amazing man. He brought out the best in her.

He nuzzled her cheek. "I'm the luckiest man here. And the happiest."

"How soon do you suppose we could sneak upstairs and do some real celebrating?" she asked and he cast her a sizzling smile. It was, after all, their one-year anniversary. And though there had been hard times and sad times, they had so much to celebrate. So much to be thankful for. Two healthy and gorgeous children, a family who loved and supported them.

And better yet, they had each other.

* * * * *

COMING NEXT MONTH

Available October 12, 2010

#2041 ULTIMATUM: MARRIAGE
Ann Major
Man of the Month

#2042 TAMING HER BILLIONAIRE BOSS
Maxine Sullivan
Dynasties: The Jarrods

#2043 CINDERELLA & THE CEO
Maureen Child
Kings of California

#2044 FOR THE SAKE OF THE SECRET CHILD
Yvonne Lindsay
Wed at Any Price

#2045 SAVED BY THE SHEIKH!
Tessa Radley

#2046 FROM BOARDROOM TO WEDDING BED?
Jules Bennett

REQUEST YOUR FREE BOOKS!

2 FREE NOVELS PLUS 2 FREE GIFTS!

Passionate, Powerful, Provocative!

Police chief Juliette Tremblant recognized the shape of the
man strolling down the street—in as calm and leisurely
fashion as if it were the middle of the day rather than
midnight. She slowed her car, convinced her eyes were
playing tricks on her. It had been a long time since Tyler
O'Neill had been seen in this town.

As she pulled to a stop at the curb, he turned toward her,
and her heart about stopped.

"What the hell are you doing here, Tyler?"

"Well, if it isn't Juliette Tremblant." He made his way
over to her, then leaned down so he could look her in the
eye. He was close enough to touch.

Juliette was not, repeat, *not* going to touch Tyler O'Neill.
Not with her fingers. Not with a ten-foot pole. There would
be no touching. Which was too bad, since it was the only
way she was ever going to convince herself the man standing
in front of her—as rumpled and heart-stoppingly handsome
now as he'd been at sixteen—was real.

And not a figment of all her furious revenge dreams.

"What are you doing back in Bonne Terre?" she asked.

"The manor is sitting empty," Tyler said and shrugged,
as though his arriving out of the blue after ten years was
casual. "Seems like someone should be watching over the
family home."

"You?" She laughed at the very notion of him being here
for any unselfish reason. "Please."

He stared at her for a second, then smiled. Her heart fluttered against her chest—a small mechanical bird powered by that smile.

"You're right." But that cryptic comment was all he offered.

Juliette bit her lip against the other questions.

Why did you go?

Why didn't you write? Call?

What did I do?

But what would be the point? Ten years of silence were all the answer she really needed.

She had sworn off feeling anything for this man long ago. Yet one look at him and all the old hurt and rage resurfaced as though they'd been waiting for the chance. That made her mad.

She put the car in gear, determined not to waste another minute thinking about Tyler O'Neill. "Have a good night, Tyler," she said, liking all the cool "go screw yourself" she managed to fit into those words.

It seems Juliette has an old score to settle with Tyler.
Pick up TYLER O'NEILL'S REDEMPTION
to see how he makes it up to her.
Available September 2010,
only from Harlequin Superromance.

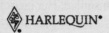
HARLEQUIN®
INTRIGUE®

Five brothers, one mystery

JOANNA WAYNE

brings an all-new suspenseful series of five
brothers searching for the truth behind their
mother's murder and their father's unknown past.

Will their journey allow them
to uncover the truth and open their hearts?

Find out in the first installment:

COWBOY SWAGGER

Available September 2010

Look for more
SONS OF TROY LEDGER
stories coming soon!